The Christmas Angel of Blue River
S. J. Bowen

Distributed by Smashwords

Discover other Books by S.J. Bowen
Time Canyon
Gone Fishing

This book is dedicated to my wife. She has encouraged and guided me over the last 40 years. She loves Christmas and Christmas stories. Our family has many Christmas traditions, including watching Christmas movies. Maybe this will be a movie someday.

Thank you, my Love!

THE CHRISTMAS ANGEL OF BLUE RIVER

First edition. February 18, 2024.

Copyright © 2024 S.J. Bowen.

ISBN: 979-8224435289

Written by S.J. Bowen.

The Christmas Angel of Blue River

CHAPTER 1

The room was dark with the flames from a flickering fire flashing off the walls. Colin Wade sat in his study just staring at the fire and dreaming of better times. Visions of his beautiful wife Lynn and the good times they had kept bouncing around in his head. He loved his wife, she loved him. They had the perfect life. Colin owned an investment company. His wife ran a successful modeling agency. Colin sold his company four years ago so he could spend more time with his wife. They loved to travel, but because of his business they were limited, with only two vacations in their ten years of marriage.

Once Colin sold his business, he said to himself that he had enough money to take care of them for more years than they could live. Colin is a billionaire, he wanted to enjoy life now, so they began to travel the world. They were able to travel in luxury and enjoy the best services. After a few months of travel, Colin needed to return home to deal with some business issues. Lynn was in the process of selling her business and could work on getting the details finalized. Their home was a large French Villa they purchased when his business became successful. They hired a butler, Williams, to help with the day-to-day running of the house. Williams was a trusted part of the family.

Suddenly his deep thoughts were interrupted.

"Dinner is served," Williams stated as he entered the room.

"Yes, Williams, I will be right there," Colin replied.

It was Thanksgiving, a favorite holiday for Colin and Lynn. As he walked to the dinner table more thoughts rushed into his head. The spot where Lynn would sit was empty.

Colin was at a meeting in New York when a call came on his cell phone, it was Williams. Colin thought it to be unusual for him to call knowing he was in meetings. Colin excused himself from the meeting and answered the call.

"Mr. Colin," Williams asked?

"Yes", Colin answered.

"Mrs. Wade has been in a car accident," Williams said.

The phone went quiet. "Sir, are you there," Williams asked?

"What happened Williams," Colin asked?

"I don't know sir; the State Police called and told me she was in an accident and taken to the hospital"

"I am heading home right now," Colin stated as he hung up the phone.

Colin could not get there fast enough. His jet landed at the little private airport and a car was waiting. In ten minutes, he was at the hospital. He asked the nurse where his wife might be, and she told him to have a seat and wait for the doctor. A half hour later a man in scrubs came into the room. He walked to Colin and stood there for a moment.

"Are you Mr. Wade," he asked?

"Yes, how is my wife?"

Colin could see the despair on his face. "Your wife passed away from her injuries." The doctor stated. "We worked on her for over an hour, but there was too much damage, I am so sorry for your loss."

Colin sat back down on the chair and put his hands over his face and began to cry. Williams came into the room and sat beside Colin.

"Sir we need to go home. We can come back tomorrow and make arrangements for her."

That was almost four years ago on Thanksgiving. Colin has been in a funk since then. Williams has been by his side every day. The loss of his wife has taken a toll on his will to live. He has not left the grounds of his house since the accident. The holidays were approaching, Williams worried about his boss and friend. He has tried to get Colin to get some help. He has refused to leave the house. The holidays were extremely hard for Colin, a dark time without his wife.

The following morning Colin sat at the small table in the kitchen and sipped on a cup of coffee. As usual, Williams brought the newspaper in and laid it on the table.

"How are you this morning," Williams asked?

"I am good," Colin responded.

Colin opened the paper and began to glance at the pages. It was the usual stuff murder, mayhem, hate. He wondered what his wife would think about the shape of the world. She was a woman with a big heart. She gave to many charities over the years. Suddenly he had a thought, I know how I can keep her memory going. He jumped from the table with a spark Williams had not seen for years.

Colin walked into his bedroom and started to change his clothes. He looked at his closet and realized he only had dress clothes, shirts, ties, sport coats, and suits. He thought for a moment then walked to the back of the house and out to a barn storage shed in the back of the estate. He remembered the gardeners would change their clothes here. He walked into the musty dark room. There were tools and mowers as well as many other gardening tools. In the back corner he saw overalls and other clothes hanging on hooks on the wall. He went through the clothes and picked out the best he could find. He folded a one-hundred-dollar bill and left it in the place where the clothes were.

He returned to the house and gave the clothes to Williams.

"Would you get these washed please," he said.

Williams looked curiously, "Sir if you need clothes, we can go into town tomorrow."

"I need these tonight," Colin said.

Williams looked concerned, "What are you planning on, sir.

"I don't know Williams. I am just thinking as I go."

Williams took the clothes and left the room. Colin went to a small room off the bedroom where a safe was kept. He quickly entered the combination and opened the door. The safe contained family valuables as well as cash. He took one stack of bills and shut the door. Money never controlled his life. He remembers when he didn't have any money and how his life was simple. Even now, he was a billionaire, money did not mean happiness. Yes, it meant he could do anything he wanted, but it didn't dictate his life.

Colin walked to his study and began to write instructions for Williams.

"Sir is there something you need?" Williams stated as he entered the room.

"Yes, I am writing this, so you have power of Attorney if something happens to me." Colin said as he signed the document. "I have contacted my attorney and advised him of my actions."

"But sir, I don't understand?"

"I will be out of touch for a while. I am not sure when I will be back."

"Where are you going Mr. C?"

"I want to find my life." Colin said with a blank face. "I need to get my life back. I know I will find it, but I don't know where."

Williams looked at the document and left it on the desk. "Sir, what is this all about?"

"I need this, Williams. I need to find myself. I need to get my life back. Lynn would want me to move forward. I don't know how, but I need to get away for a while."

Williams looked concerned, "sir is there something I can do?"

"No William, but I am taking my cell phone so I will stay in touch."

Williams left the room and Colin went about getting dressed. He is a handsome man six-foot-two, light brown hair and a lean physique. Not bad for a man in his early forties. The clothes fit a little loose but would do. He thought I can get some other clothes in town.

He looked in the mirror, "I look like a ragamuffin." He thought.

It was getting late, he wanted to get started. Colin lived in New England, in an area where many wealthy people live. He wanted to get away and find quiet and peace. He thought he would look for people who needed help. He needed to be anonymous and stealthy. This is something Lynn would be happy with.

Colin called a cab and went to the front door and waited.

"Sir, I am concerned," Williams stated with a worried look.

"Don't worry Williams, I will stay in touch. No one knows what I am doing. Okay?"

"Yes Sir, I will take care of everything while you are gone. I will worry until you come home."

"Williams this is something I need to do for my sanity."

The doorbell rang and Colin walked to the door. He turned and shook Williams' hand and walked out the door to the waiting cab.

CHAPTER 2

The cab driver opened the door for Colin. He had no luggage.

"Do you have any bags sir?" the driver asked.

"No just me." Colin smiled.

The driver shut the door and jumped into the driver's seat. "Where to sir?"

Colin took a one-hundred-dollar bill out and said, "how far will this go?"

The driver took the bill and drove off. The sights were new since he had not been out of the house for over three years. The trees whizzed by as they sped down the road. Soon they came to the highway crossing.

"Which way would you like to go," the driver pointed at the sign.

"Heads it's north, tails it is south," Colin said taking a coin from his pocket.

Up went the coin, "Heads, I guess it's North," exclaimed Colin.

The driver steered the cab north and up the highway they went. Colin was still watching the sights as they drove. It has changed a lot since I was here last, he thought. I wish Lynn was with me, she would have loved this adventure.

It had been more than an hour Colin wondered where they were.

"Where are we?"

"We are near the town of Blue River," the driver said.

"That sounds nice," Colin responded. "I think we can stop there."

The driver took the next offramp and soon Colin could see the main street. It was all lit up with Christmas decorations.

"You can let me out here. I think I will walk the rest of the way," Colin said as he pointed to the curb.

"Are you sure sir?" the driver said. "It is dark here and if I go a little further it is much brighter."

"No this will be fine," Colin stated as he exited the cab.

Colin reached into his pocket and pulled out another One-hundred-dollar bill and handed it to the driver.

"This is too much sir," the driver said.

"You keep it and have a safe drive back," Colin said as he walked away.

Colin could see the beautiful Christmas decorations just up the street a few blocks. This will get me in the mood he thought. Just then a dark figure came out of the shadows.

"I need your money," the shadow said.

"Do I look like I have money?" Colin replied.

"You just got out of a cab. I know you have some money," the shadow replied.

Colin squinted to try to see the dark figure. Suddenly, he was shoved from behind. He fell to the ground into the dirt.

Give us your money or we will beat it out of you," the voice said.

Suddenly, there was a light from an oncoming car. It shined on both men, they ducked and ran back into the shadows. The car was a police car. It slowly went by Colin on the ground. They passed and continued up the street. Colin took the opportunity to get up and run toward the main streetlights. He slowed and stopped to brush the dirt off his clothes. He thought he must look like a homeless person. He walked up the street and saw a Diner up ahead. As he got close, he noticed it was open. He walked through the door and was greeted by a very pretty waitress.

"Welcome to Dan's Diner," she said with a smile.

"Thanks," Colin replied.

"Just sit anywhere," she pointed to the open booths.

Colin looked around the room. There were two young kids, a boy, and a girl, sitting in a booth near the door, otherwise the place was empty. Colin sat in a booth near the kitchen. He could see the decorations on the street, and he thought it was beautiful. The waitress came over to him to get his order.

"What can I get for you?" she asked.

Colin only had one-hundred-dollar bills in his pocket. He had three quarters in his pocket and figured coffee was the only thing he could order.

"I will have a cup of coffee please," he said looking at the waitress.

She looked at him and thought, another homeless guy that won't have any money. She smiled and went into the back room. Just then the two young people jumped up and ran out of the diner. Colin got up and went to the door and watched as the two disappeared down the street. He looked down and noticed the check was on the table and no money in it. He quickly took out a one-hundred-dollar bill and put it on the table. The waitress came around the corner and noticed Colin standing there. "Where did they go?" she asked.

"They just got up and left," Colin answered.

The waitress walked over to the table with a disgusted look, figuring the two had did the dine and dash. She looked down at the table and noticed a bill under the check. She smiled and took the check and the cash to the register. She took the change from the large bill and put it in her pocket. Colin went back to his booth and sat. The waitress poured coffee in a cup and moved to the table. Colin looked down so she would not think he was watching her.

"Here you go," she said as she put the coffee on the table along with a big piece of pie.

"I didn't order pie," he said.

"It's okay, I just got a big tip," she said with a big smile. "I don't usually get big tips here."

"That is great," Colin replied, as he took a bite of pie.

"You are new here?" she asked. "I have never seen you before and I know most of the locals."

"I am just wandering through," Colin responded.

"Well do you have a place to stay. If not, I may have a proposition for you."

She walked into the kitchen area and came out with a large man.

"This is Dan, he owns the joint," the waitress said as she pointed to the man.

Colin stood up and shook his hand, "Nice to meet you, I am Colin."

Dan looked at Colin and said, "Nice to meet you. Did you just roll in the dirt?"

"Ha, no sir I just had an encounter with two gentlemen outside of town," Colin responded looking at his dirty clothes.

"Well as Mary told you, I have a proposition for you. My dishwasher just up and disappeared. I need a dishwasher. It pays $7.00 an hour and three meals a day if you want. I will let you stay in the room out back of the diner. It is nice and clean."

Colin looked at Dan and then at Mary, "Well it's hard to turn that down.

Dan smiled, "You start tomorrow at six a.m. Is that good?"

Colin smiled, "that will be great. Don't you need someone now?"

Dan looked at the half-eaten pie and said, "Finish your pie and then I will show you around."

Colin sat back down and took another bite of pie. Mary came over to him, "I am Mary, Mary Wells."

Colin stood up and put his hand out, "I am Colin Wade."

"Well Colin it looks like we will be working together. Dan is a nice guy; he is like a second father to me. When my parents died a few years ago he took me under his wing. If you follow me, I will take you to your room.

Colin got up and followed Mary through the kitchen and out the back door to a small shed-like structure. She opened the door, they walked in, "Well it's not much but it is warm and clean."

Colin smiled and looked around. There was a small bathroom with a shower, a small sink with a coffee maker next to it and a queen size bed. "This is nice, I appreciate doing this. I wasn't sure where I was going to stay tonight."

Mary smiled, "Good I am glad things worked out."

They both walked back to the kitchen and Colin watched as Dan cleaned the cook top. Colin moved over to the dishwasher and began loading it with dishes.

Dan looked over, "You know you don't have to do that right now. I will finish it up."

Colin smiled and looked over at Dan, "I know, I figured I might as well get a head start on things."

Dan smiled and went back to work on the kitchen. Soon Mary came into the kitchen, "We are all closed up."

Colin looked at his watch; it was eleven o'clock. Wow, where did the day go? Mary took off her apron and put on her sweater.

"I am out of here Dan," she exclaimed.

"Okay, see you in the morning. We have a big day tomorrow," Dan said as he continued to clean the kitchen.

Colin finished his work and told Dan good night, then went to his room. I don't have any other clothes than these. I will need to get a change of clothes tomorrow. He hung his clothes on a hook by the bed and jumped into the shower. He dried off and crawled into bed. Boy, am I tired he thought; tomorrow is another day in his big adventure.

Colin woke to the sweet smell of bacon. He got up and splashed water on his face and took his clothes off the hook. He shook them out as if that might help them look better. I have no toothbrush, no deodorant, nothing. Oh well he thought, I will pick up some things today. Colin walked into the kitchen and looked around. There were four men in the kitchen, but no Dan.

"Hi, I am Colin," he said as he walked in. "Where is Dan?" Just then Dan walked into the kitchen.

"Hey, good morning, how did you sleep?"

"I slept like a baby. I must have been tired." Colin replied.

Dan walked over to put his hand on his shoulder, "This is Colin. He will be our busboy to replace that piece of shit that left us high and dry. These guys are my cook crew. The guy over there is Frank, the guy over by the grill is Ed, the guy over next to the fridge is Rick, and finally this guy is Bill. They all work different shifts, but today we all work together. We will be terribly busy today and we will be closing at six o'clock."

Colin looked dazed, "Okay, I guess I will try to remember all your names. Why are we expecting a big day?"

"Tonight, we have the town tree lighting. Just about everyone will be there. Since we are closing early, people will be in early to eat before the ceremony. The ceremony is at seven sharp, I think you will enjoy it." Dan said as he moved Colin toward a small table in the kitchen. "I want you to sit here and eat." Dan slid a plate onto the table. "Here is a new dish, I want you to try it."

Colin looked at the plate, "Looks like eggs benedict."

"You got it. It is a new recipe. I have been trying to perfect this for a long time. Hope you like it."

Colin took a bite and then another, "wow that is the best I have ever tasted. I have had many of these in my travels."

Dan smiled and turned to the other cooks, "See I knew we found the right recipe."

Colin finished his breakfast and sipped the last of his coffee. He walked into the dining area and noticed three waitresses talking to each other. "Hi I am Colin. I am your busboy."

They turned and looked at him, "Hi, I am Laura, "said the youngest, who was at least ten years older than him. "This is Kay," she pointed to the woman with the red hair. "Jane here is married to Rick the cook. Mary will be here later."

"Hi all, I met Mary last night. Nice to meet you all. Let me know if you need my help." Colin replied as he walked toward the group.

"Where did Dan get this guy?" Mumbled Jane. "The last guy was an ass. He wouldn't help with anything. This guy is a breath of fresh air."

"Okay let's open!" Dan yelled from the back.

Colin walked to the back and dawned his apron. I am ready, he thought. It has been years since I have had a real job. The door was open, and people were streaming in, soon all the tables were full. The girls went about their business-like pros. Soon the first table was open. Colin went about clearing the dishes.

"Honey if you do it this way it will be easier," Kay stated as she showed him how to stack the dishes.

"Thank you," Colin replied. "I appreciate the help."

The morning was terribly busy, and Colin was having a hard time keeping up. He knew he needed to clear the tables off so they could get more people in. He would move to the kitchen and get the dishwasher full and then scrub the pots. The girls would help by bringing dishes to him. There was a lull for about twenty minutes, and he was able to catch up. Soon Mary walked into the back room and put her apron on.

"Did you stop to see him on your way?" Dan asked.

"Yes, he was in good spirits. He wants so bad to see the tree lighting. The doctor said it would not be advisable." Mary answered.

Colin wondered who she was talking about. A parent, maybe a friend, maybe a boyfriend. He thought it is none of his business. He kept looking at Mary and thought what a beautiful woman she was. She reminded him of Lynn in a lot of ways.

The day was going fast, Colin was proud that he was keeping up. It was about two o'clock and he could not believe it was that late.

There was a tap on his shoulder, "okay, you have had enough fun for the day. My late guy should be in soon. Take this," Dan held out his hand with some cash in it.

"What is this?" Colin asked.

"Let's call it an advance. I want you to go get some work clothes and most of all get some good work shoes. Two blocks down is the General Store, ask for Jed, he is the owner. Tell him I sent you." Dan smiled.

Colin looked at the man he had only met yesterday and could not believe he was doing this. "I will pay you back for everything. I appreciate this."

Dan pointed to the back door, "Get going, I will see you at the tree lighting."

Colin smiled and walked to the door. He went to his room and washed his face and hands. He grabbed his money and his phone and walked out to the street. Okay, Dan said it was two blocks up the street. He slowly walked up the street. It was beautiful, everything was decorated and festive. Every shop had decorations in the window and outside. Soon he saw the General Store. It was lit up like the other stores and it had a large tree out front. It looked like it had just about everything he needed. He walked into the store; wow it was amazing. A little bit of everything. He approached the man at the counter, "Hi, I am Colin. Dan sent me over."

"Well, hi there young man, I am Jed. What can I do for you?"

Jed was a tall slender black man. His hair was gray, he had a big smile.

"Well, I need a few things. Let's start with pants and shirts," Colin said as he looked around.

Jed led Colin to the back of the store, and they began to go through the clothes. An hour later, Colin had a pile of clothes and shoes. He walked to the front counter where Jed was finishing with another customer.

"Well young man, did you find everything?"

"I found everything and more," Colin laughed. "I need something to put all of these in; Do you have something?"

Jed pointed to a stack of duffel bags. Colin walked over and picked up a bag and walked back to the counter. "This will do just fine."

"Okay, you said Dan sent you?"

"Yes, I am working for him right now."

"Okay son, that means you get the Blue River discount."

"Oh, that's nice of you."

Jed looked at Colin, "So what happened to all your clothes?"

Colin thought someone might ask that question, "Well, the place I was staying burnt down with all my stuff. I collected my last paycheck and started walking."

"That's too bad. Hopefully, you will have better luck here."

Colin thanked Jed for his help and walked back to his room. A shower and a shave made him feel better. On with the new clothes and everything was set. He figured he had some time before the tree lighting, so he would explore the town.

He could not get over how festive everything was. Every store and office had lights. Beautiful lights hung across the street and hung from the streetlights. She walked up the street and he noticed a store called the Emporium, so he decided to take a look. It said there was antiques and gifts. It was beautifully decorated. He pushed the door open and was immediately greeted like he was with Jed.

"Hi there, welcome to the Emporium. Is there anything I can help you with?" Said the gray-haired woman behind the counter.

"Thank you, but I think I'll just look for a bit."

"That is fine, if you need anything just ask. My name is Millie."

Colin began to wander through the store. Boy my wife would have loved this place. She loved antiques, that's why our home was filled with them. The place was full of beautiful gifts and jewelry. It is too bad he didn't have anybody to give them to, he thought.

He looked at his watch; he had about a half hour before the lighting. He moved to leave and pushed the door open.

"Are you going to the tree lighting?" Millie asked.

"Yes, I will be there."

"I will see you there," she said.

Collin walked out the door and began to walk up the street. He could hear Christmas carols in the distance. He walked toward the sound. It was a little town square with a grassy area in the middle. A gazebo in the center with a choir singing songs. There were small booths all around selling everything for Christmas. This is out of a Christmas dream. This town knew how to celebrate Christmas. There was a giant pine tree near the front of the green area. It had to be forty feet tall. This must be the tree. He could smell the hot cocoa being served in one of the booths. As he looked toward the booth, he noticed Mary walking up to him.

CHAPTER 3

"Hi Mary."

"Hi Colin, glad to see you were able to make it."

"I wouldn't miss it. This is beautiful. All the decorations and the smells. Speaking of smells, would you like some hot cocoa?"

"Oh, that would be great. Extra marshmallows!"

"I love extra marshmallows."

Colin returned with two hot cocoa specials. Good timing because an announcement called everybody to the tree for the lighting. A man stepped up to the mic and made an introduction.

"Ladies and gentlemen, boys and girls, I would like to introduce our Mayor, Millie Taylor."

Everybody began to clap, a woman walked onto the podium.

"Hey, that is the lady who owns the Emporium!" Colin announced.

"Yes, she is our mayor too. She is a wonderful mayor. She is always trying to bring new business to our town."

The mayor had everybody count down the tree lighting. "Three, two, one, Merry Christmas!"

The tree was beautiful. The lights and ornaments looked perfect, then everybody began to sing Christmas carols. After two more carols everybody cheered and began to wander around the square.

"Well, I need to go see Wil for a while."

"Wil?" Colin asked.

"Oh, I guess you wouldn't know about him. Wil is my son. He is in the hospital. He has a heart problem. The Doctor said he has a congenital heart issue. He said they can fix it, but my insurance only covers so much. I also need to take him to Texas for surgery. I can't afford that, so we are waiting to see if we can get a doctor to come here. He is so disappointed that he couldn't make it to the tree lighting. He has not missed one since he was born."

"So, you don't know when the doctor might get here?"

"My insurance is not particularly good. They said it might take some time, but it will happen. We just don't know when."

"I can't believe they would do such a thing." Colin shook his head and then decided he was going to do something about the situation.

"Would you like to come with me and meet Wil?"

"I would love to meet your son."

The hospital was just around the corner. It had only twenty beds, but it was just a small town, so it was a good fit. They walked into the hospital and down the hall to Wil's room. Wil smiled when he saw his mom.

"Hi mom, how was the tree lighting?" Wil asked.

"It was beautiful as usual. I am sorry you could not be there. This is Colin. He is a friend from work."

"Hi, nice to meet you. So how come you're not outside playing?"

"The doctor said I have this thing in my heart, I can't play until it is fixed."

Colin smiled at Wil. "Well, have you ever heard of the Christmas Angel?"

"The Christmas Angel?" Wil asked.

"The Christmas Angel comes only at Christmas time. They look for someone who has been good and needs help. They look around the world for those who pray for their help."

Mary glanced at Colin then looked at Wil. "Yes, you need to pray hard to get their attention."

Wil looked at his mother, "I guess I need to pray for a Christmas Angel."

"Wil, I need to go home. I work the early shift tomorrow." Mary said.

"Ok, will I see you tomorrow?"

"Yes, I will be here."

"Can I come by and visit too?" Colin asked.

"Yes, we can talk about the Christmas Angel.

Mary and Colin walked out of the hospital and down the street.

"Thanks for making him feel happy. He was sad because he missed the tree lighting."

Colin smiled, "My pleasure. Can I walk you home?"

"No, I will be all right. And I am just down the street. You need to get some sleep too. You are working the early shift too."

Colin waved at Mary as the went their own way. Colin knew he had to work quick to get things arranged for tomorrow. He went to his room and grabbed his phone and dialed Williams.

"Hello, Mr. Colin"

"Hi Williams, how is everything there?"

"We are doing well sir. How are you?"

"I am well Williams. I have a job for you."

"Yes sir, what can I do?"

"I need you to call Dr. Jacobs tonight. I have a young boy here that needs his help. He has a heart problem; he can't wait any longer. Let him know the boy is in room 133. His name is Wil Wells. I want him to take care of Wil. Let him know that if he does this, he will get another million dollars for his hospital. Do you have all of that Williams?"

"Yes sir."

"One other thing contact the hospital and tell them to send all bills to my attorney. I will let him know it is coming. This is all to be done anonymously. No one must know where the money is coming from. I will contact you tomorrow to make sure there are no problems."

"I think I understand sir. I will get right on this. Sir, are you sure you are all right?"

"Williams, I am doing fine. I feel better than I have felt in a long time."

Colin hung up the phone and called his attorney and filled him in on the situation. He felt good as he laid down on his bed. I hope this all works, he thought. Soon he dozed off.

Again, Colin was awakened by the smell of food cooking. After a quick shower and shave, he dressed and walked into the restaurant. "Boy something smells good."

Dan looked up at Colin, "Go have a seat. I have a treat for you." Dan brought a plate of what looked like pancakes.

"Ok, what is this?"

Dan smiled, "These are crepes filled with crab and covered with my secret sauce. I am trying another new recipe."

Colin took a bite; wow is this good he thought. "Dan, this is delicious, are you going to add it to the menu?"

"No, I have been experimenting with recipes for a few years. I had hoped to open a white tablecloth restaurant for some time."

Colin took another bite, "How come you haven't done it?"

"I can't get financing. I have contacted just about every bank for miles. They say a restaurant is too big a risk."

Colin finished the dish, "Boy was that good. I know a guy who invests in this type of thing. I took care of his estate while he was out of town. He told me that if I ever came across a good investment to let him know."

Dan chuckled, "You have a friend with money?"

"I know it is hard to believe, your dishwasher knows someone with money. If it is okay, I will give him a call."

Dan smiled, "Sure I guess it won't hurt."

Colin finished and washed his dishes. The doors were about to open, but Mary was not there. I hope everything is all right. Just then Dan walked into the room.

"Mary will not be here for the next few days. It looks like a doctor has come to help with Wil. They may be able to do surgery in the next few days if all goes well."

Colin hid a smile, "That is good news."

"Very good news." Dan responded, "That means I will need you to do double duty. I have called Jane in to take Mary's place, but she won't be here for an hour our so."

"I don't know how to wait tables."

"You can do it." Dan replied. "I will help."

Colin grabbed a sales book and changed his apron, then opened the door. It was a rough hour. Colin needed to explain each order to the cooks. He didn't know how to write the orders so the cooks could understand.

Jane came in and immediately went to work.

"Boy, am I glad to see you."

"I got here as soon as I could. Are you doing all right?" Jane asked.

"I am tired, but I can catch up now."

Colin worked hard for the remaining shift. He was anxious to get to the hospital.

Chapter 4

Colin finished his shift and quickly showered and changed. He immediately walked across the street to the General Store. He was greeted by Jed as he walked in the door.

"Hi, Colin. What can I do for you?"

"Hi, Jed. I am looking for a very small Christmas tree, some miniature lights, and ornaments."

"The only trees I have are those in the lot next door. The only lights and ornaments are large and made for big trees and outdoors. However, I know Millie has some at the Emporium."

"Thank Jed, I will head over there."

Colin walked into the Emporium and Millie greeted him. "Hi Colin, how are you?"

"Hi Mayor, I am just fine."

"Please, just Millie."

"Okay Millie, I need your help. I am looking for a miniature Christmas tree with all the lights and ornaments."

"Okay let's go over here. Is this what you are looking for?"

"Oh, that is a prefect tree."

"Is this for you?"

"No Millie. It is for a little boy in the hospital."

"That little boy might be Wil?"

"Yes, how did you now?"

"Many of us here know about the boy's problem. We have been trying to help any way we can."

"Wow, that is great. Now we need some lights and ornaments."

Millie gathered everything and placed it on the counter. "That will be ten dollars."

"Ten dollars? That can't be."

"I am covering the tree and ornaments; you can get the lights."

"You don't need to do that."

"I want to help."

"Well thanks. I will let him know you are thinking of him. By the way, is there an electronics store in town?"

"Yes, if you go across the street and down two blocks."

"Can I leave these bags here until I come back?"

"Sure, they will be right here when you come back."

Colin jogged across the street and disappeared into the electronics store. Soon, he came out with a small Christmas package. Back to the Emporium, he grabbed the bags and thanked Millie again then went out the door. He walked quickly to the hospital and then to Wil's room. "Hi there young Wil!"

Wil quickly looked up then smiled. "Hi Colin, I was hoping you would come by."

"Where is your mom?"

"She went to get something to eat. She will be back soon."

Colin lifted the bags up to the table next to the bed. "Since you couldn't be at the tree lighting, I brought it to you." Colin pulled the tree out of the bag and set it on the tray on the bed. Then he pulled the lights out and the ornaments.

Wil's face lit up. "Wow that is cool."

"Okay, let's get started on decorating this tree."

Just then a man walked into the room. It is Dr. Jacobs. "Well how are we doing?"

"We are just fine," answered Colin.

"Can I see you outside?" Dr. Jacobs inquired.

"Sure. I will be back in a minute Wil, you keep decorating."

Colin walked out of the room with Dr. Jacobs.

"Ok, I know you don't want anyone to know you have anything to do with this, but I needed to talk to you."

Colin looked around, "Let's go in this room. Okay what do you think?"

"Well, I have looked at everything the hospital has, based on what I see it should be an easy surgery. However, I need to have an MRI done."

"Okay, let's get it done." Colin responded.

"Well, they don't have an MRI machine here. The closest on is one hundred miles from here."

"Okay what do we do now?"

Dr. Jacobs smiled, "Well I have ordered a portable MRI machine to be here tomorrow."

"They have portable MRI machines?"

"Yes, they are in a big semi-trailer. It is going to cost you eighty-thousand-dollars."

"Wow, I guess it needed to be done."

"Well, that is not all. I ordered a new MRI machine for the hospital. It is part of the deal I have with the hospital for letting me work here. Don't ask what it costs."

Colin smirked, "I figured you had something else up your sleeve."

"That's not all. Instead of the one million you pledged, you owe a two-million-dollar donation to my hospital."

Colin scratched his head. "I guess you got me. You do promise me that you can fix Wil?"

"I think he is going to be just fine. The surgery will be simple. I will not need to open him up. He will be up and running in a week."

Colin smiled, "That's good news. I need to get back before his mom gets back."

Colin left Dr. Jacobs and returned to Wil's room. "Wow you are almost finished with the tree. Here I have two batteries for the lights. Let's wait for your mom to turn them on."

"Okay, but I found this." Will held up the Christmas wrapped package."

"All right, it is an early Christmas present. Go ahead and open it."

Will started to tear the paper off the package. "Oh my, it is a computer tablet. Just what I wanted."

Colin grinned, "I am glad you like it. I had some games loaded on the tablet."

Mary walked into the room, "What is going on here?"

"Look mom, Colin brought me a Christmas tree. We decorated it and put the lights on it. We waited for you to turn it on."

"Very nice."

Colin moved to the light switch, "Okay I will turn the lights off and you two count down the tree lighting."

Colin turned the lights off and they began to count down the numbers. On the count of one Wil turned the tree lights on.

Mary smiled, "Very nice. Thank you, Colin."

"My pleasure."

"Look mom, I got an early Christmas present."

Mary looked at Colin, "You are too generous."

"He is stuck here without much to do. I figured he needed something to occupy his time."

For the next two hours they talked and enjoyed each other's company.

Mary stood up, "It is time for you to go to sleep and time for us to go home."

Wil smiled and begrudgingly said, "Okay."

Colin and Mary walked out of the room and out of the hospital.

"Mary, I will walk you home."

'Oh, that's not necessary."

"You are just down the street from me, so it is not a problem."

"I appreciate it. Why are you here?"

"Well, after my wife died, I was in a funk. I thought doing some traveling and getting out would do me some good. I saw your little town and thought it might be a nice place to stop. How did you get here?"

"My husband's work brought us here. He got a job at a law firm down the road a few miles. We liked this little town and decided to settle here. We were going to buy a house soon. When he died, he didn't have any insurance, so Wil and I were left with nothing. He had a massive heart attack at work. I was devastated and I had nothing. I had to take a job at Dan's. He has been so good to me and Wil."

They arrived at Mary's apartment and Colin noticed a beat-up older car. "Is that your car?"

"Well, it was. It doesn't run anymore. It is a hopeless cause. Even if I had the money, it wouldn't be worth it." Would you like to come in for some coffee?"

"I would like that."

They walked into the front door; Colin noticed a sparsely decorated living room. A small couch, an old chair, and a coffee table. He followed Mary into the kitchen that contained a table for two. Mary walked to the coffee pot and began to prepare the coffee. She opened the refrigerator and there was hardly any food or drinks in the empty appliance.

"Would you like some milk in your coffee?"

"No thanks, just black. Where is Wil's room?"

"It is just down the hall on the left."

Colin walked into Wil's room; it was almost as sparse as the living room. There was a poster of the New York Rangers on the wall. He walked back to the kitchen.

"Wil is a hockey fan?"

"Oh, he is a big hockey fan. He loves the Rangers."

"I am a big hockey fan too. Maybe when he is better, we can get to a game."

Colin finished his coffee and stood up, "I should be going. I know where you will be tomorrow. Keep us informed. Everybody is concerned. You know, if you give me your key, I can have some supper ready for you when you come home from the hospital."

Mary walked to a drawer and retrieved a key. "Here, it is. I would appreciate having a meal when I get home. I am usually very tired and just go to bed."

Colin took the key, "I will see you tomorrow. Oh, by the way, I bought you a ticket to the new car giveaway. The drawing is tomorrow."

"Thanks Colin. I never win those things."

Colin walked back to his room behind the restaurant and retrieved his phone. He dialed Williams. "Williams this is Colin."

"Yes sir, are you all right?"

"I am fine. I am having a great time here. I have another job for you."

"Yes, sir."

"I need you to get ahold of Kathy and ask her to meet me here tomorrow at Dan's Diner at three o'clock."

"What should I tell her, sir?"

"Just tell her I need her to help me help someone."

"Yes, sir."

"Williams, I want you to go to the car dealer and buy the nicest SUV they have. I don't care what it costs, have it delivered to the address I give you. Again, nobody must know where it came from. A note goes with it saying, you are the winner of the new car giveaway."

"Sir, I will take care of it."

Chapter 5

Colin woke up to his alarm. I have a lot to do today, I better get started. He grabbed his phone and dialed. He cleared his throat and disguised his voice.

"Hello, is this Dan Baxter?"

"Yes, it is."

"Hi Dan, I am Bruce Crawford. Colin Wade called me to let me know that you needed an investor for your restaurant."

"Well thank you. Yes, I am looking for an investor."

"How much are you looking for Dan?"

"Well, don't you want to know what I am going to do with it?"

"Colin told me about your restaurant idea. He said you are an outstanding chef."

"Okay, well, I need around five hundred thousand dollars."

"Will that make it easy to complete?"

"Well, I originally figured it would cost eight hundred thousand dollars, but I can do it with five."

"Dan, it would my pleasure to invest in your dream. I will send over some paperwork for you to review. If it is good, just sign and mail them back."

"Sounds very fair Bruce. I look forward to meeting you."

Dan hung the phone up and turned with a big smile.

Colin hid his phone and walked into the restaurant. Dan immediately grabbed him and gave him a hug.

"What is that for?"

"I just got a call from Bruce Crawford. He is going to invest in my restaurant!"

"Oh, great. He is a good guy."

"Yes, he is. He is going to send me the paperwork."

Dan went about telling everybody about his news. Colin went to work cleaning up pots and pans for the breakfast rush. It seemed like the day dragged on. Colin was anxious to get up to Mary's apartment to meet Kathy. Kathy is an assistant to his attorney. She helps Colin when he needs help. The clock finally said two-thirty. Colin told Dan he was leaving and dashed out the door. He ran up the street to Mary's place and he saw Kathy sitting in her car.

"Hi, Kathy. Thanks for being here. Come on and I will show you what I need."

They walked into Mary's apartment and Colin shut the door behind them. "I need your help making this place festive. Also, if you could go the store and stock her refrigerator. I will have some Christmas lights and a Christmas tree delivered in an hour. You think you can help me?"

"Of course. What is this all about?"

"I decided that this is something my wife Lynn would have wanted me to do. I needed to get out of my funk, this has done it."

"Okay, I assume you like this woman?"

"Well, maybe. She needs help. Her son is in the hospital waiting to have heart surgery. Her son Wil is a great little boy. So, are you up to the task?"

"I am at your service."

"Let's start by stocking the kitchen."

They investigated every cupboard and drawer, then the refrigerator. Kathy looked at Colin, "There is not much here."

"Yes, let's start with the basics. Milk, eggs, butter, and that sort of stuff. Then get the extras. The grocery store is down main street just a short distance. By the way, I told her I would have dinner ready for her, so if you can get some stuff for dinner, I would appreciate it."

Kathy laughed, "I will see what I can do."

"I am going to the General Store and pick up a tree and some decorations."

They both left and went about their assignments. Colin walked to the General Store and met Jake. "Hi, Jake."

"Hi Colin, what can I do for you?"

"I need some Christmas decorations."

"Well, you have come to the right place. Let's start with lights."

They went about picking out all the best decorations. Then out to pick a tree. Once everything was gathered, they went back to the front desk.

"Colin, what are you going to do with all of this?"

"I am going to decorate Mary's place. She has been so busy taking care of Wil, she has not had time to do anything."

"You are a good person. I want to donate something, so the tree is on me. Mary is a genuinely nice person and I want to help."

"Thanks Jake. I am sure she will appreciate all of this. Can you deliver this to her place?"

"Sure, I can have it there in an hour,"

Colin quickly returned to Mary's apartment to see if there was anything he needed to do. Soon there was a knock on the door. He opened the door; it was the tree and the decorations. "Wow, that was quick."

The young man at the door asked, "Where would you like the tree, sir?"

"Right here will be fine," Colin pointed to a spot by the front window.

Colin gave the boy a ten-dollar bill, "Wow, thank you sir!"

Just then Kathy came in the door with two bags of groceries. "There are more bags in my car."

Colin went to her car and started to unload the many bags she brought. Once they were all in the kitchen Kathy went to work putting away all the goodies.

"This is fun," Kathy said as she unloaded one of the bags. "It is nice to go shopping with someone else's money. I bought everything. I also bought you some goodies for dinner."

"Oh, thank you for all of this. She should be here in about an hour. She will be surprised."

"I picked up some wine also."

"Good, I think she will like a glass of wine."

They went about filling all the cupboards and the refrigerator. Kathy looked at the tree and smiled.

"Do you need help with the tree?"

"Thanks, but no, I think Mary would like to help me do that."

Kathy picked up her purse, "Is there anything else I can do?"

"There is one more thing, I need some hockey things for Wil's room. He is a big Ranger's fan."

"I think I can do that. I have some friends at their management office."

Kathy left and Colin set the table with a candle, plates napkins and wine glasses. He went to the tree and began to place the lights on the bows. He heard the door open and looked quickly at the door.

Mary looked at Colin on the small step ladder, "What is this and what are you doing?"

"I thought I would surprise you, are you surprised?"

"Yes, I am surprised. It looks nice and smells good. I will help you decorate it."

"First we eat," Colin pointed to the kitchen.

Mary walked into the kitchen and smiled, "Oh this looks nice."

Colin pulled out the chair, "Sit and I will pour a glass of wine."

"Oh yes, I need some wine. I haven't had any for weeks. I usually come home and collapse. This is nice."

Colin poured them both a glass of wine and sat at the table. "So, what is going on at the hospital?"

"Good news. The Doctor says he will do his surgery tomorrow after noon."

"Oh, that is good news."

"I am going back later and spend the night with him. I will probably do it tomorrow too."

"Don't worry about a thing here. I will have the tree all set for when you both come home."

There was a knock on the door. Mary got up and answered it, 'Hi, can I help you?"

"Yes mam, are you Mary Wells?"

"I am, what is this all about?"

"You have won the car raffle and I have your prize."

Mary looked back at Colin, "Is this the raffle you told me about?"

Colin stood up, "Yes, I only bought one ticket. I didn't think I had a chance of winning."

Mary had a blank look, "What did I win?"

The man pointed to the street where a beautiful silver SUV was parked.

"What? Where?"

"Mam the SUV parked there," He pointed again to the street.

Mary stepped back and Colin grabbed her arm, "Let's go look at it."

They walked out of the apartment and up the SUV, "It is beautiful, are you sure it is mine?"

"Yes ma'am, here are the keys." The man stepped into his tow truck and drove down the street.

Colin opened the driver's door, "get in and check it out."

Mary stepped into the driver's seat, "I have never won anything. I can't believe this. Thank you, Colin for entering me in the raffle."

"I just thought it might cheer you up. I never win anything. I can't believe you won." Colin turned his head away and smiled.

Mary just kept looking at the new car, "I just found out that someone paid for all the medical bills. This is just too much. I just can't believe all of this."

"Well, I have to believe that it is Wil praying for the Christmas Angel. Let's go back and have our dinner."

They walked back into the apartment. Mary was still in shock. She picked up the glass of wine and took a big gulp. Colin smiled and began to serve the dinner Kathy had brought.

"Did you cook all of this."

"Oh no, I can't cook. It is from the grocery store. I just thought you would like a nice hot meal." Colin looked at Mary and realized he was feeling something for her. He had not felt this way in a long time. He bent down and kissed Mary on the cheek.

Mary looked up at him, "Thank you so much for everything. I think you are a wonderful person." Mary felt something for Colin also. She had a lot on her mind to think about her feelings.

They finished their dinner and another glass of wine. They both started to decorate the tree and enjoyed some Christmas music on the radio. Mary needed to get back to the hospital, so Colin again kissed her on the cheek, she quickly left. Colin continued to decorate the tree. He also placed lights around the front window to give a festive look. It was time to get some sleep, so Colin locked up and walked back to his room. He was happy. She didn't notice the supplies in the kitchen, so that will be another surprise. Everything went well and he believed she didn't suspect anything.

Chapter 6

Morning came too soon. Colin was not ready to get up. It was a little cool and it snowed again last night. Colin turned up the heat and jumped into the shower. After dressing he checked his phone for any messages. There was a message from Kathy. She had acquired the hockey equipment and would wait to hear from him before delivering. Colin responded, "Thank You."

Colin walked into the restaurant and noticed Dan was whistling a tune and had a big smile on his face. "Why the big smile?"

Dan turned to look at Colin. "I am simply happy. I am going to realize my dream. My new restaurant dream is going to happen. Besides, it is Christmas!"

Colin sat and ate his breakfast. Now it is time to go to work. Colin tied his apron on and began to rinse dishes. The girls out front were busy and Colin started to clear an empty table and he noticed the Sheriff at the counter eating his breakfast. Colin rinsed his dishes and placed them into the dishwasher. Back again to another empty table. Colin noticed two men standing in front of the Diner. They looked like the two men who attacked him. Colin moved to the counter where the Sheriff was sitting.

"Hi, I am Colin, how are you?"

"Hi, I am Sheriff Tom Daily. I am fine, how do you like our little town?"

"I love it here. Can I talk to you about something that happened to me here?"

"Sure, what is it?"

Colin looked back at the two men outside. "When I came into town, I was attacked by two men. A passing Sheriff's car scared them off. I think the two men standing outside are the two who attacked me."

The Sheriff turned and looked at the two men. Just then the men looked up and down the street and began to walk toward the General Store. Before entering the store, they pulled their hoods up over their heads. Sheriff Daily jumped up from the counter and quickly went out the door, with Colin close behind.

Sheriff Daily spoke into his radio, "All units, an armed robbery in progress at the General Store. I am entering the building."

Just then a shot rang out. The Sheriff drew his gun and entered the store. Colin slowly opened the door of the store. He immediately noticed Jed on the floor, bleeding from his shoulder. Colin moved quickly to Jed, grabbing a tee shirt off the counter. He placed the shirt on Jed's shoulder and began to put pressure on the wound.

"You are going to be okay Jed. Help is on the way." Colin sat next to Jed and kept pressure on the wound.

Suddenly, a shot rang out. The sound of running footsteps was coming toward them. Colin grabbed an umbrella from the container next to the counter. The footsteps came closer. Colin saw a man running toward the door. He stuck out the umbrella and the man tripped and fell into a display case, knocking him out. Colin stood up and looked for the Sheriff. Sheriff Daily came out of the back room.

"Are you okay?"

"I am fine, but the guy in the office is not."

The other deputies arrived and took over. Colin went back to Jed. "You are going to be safe now. We just need to get you to the hospital." Soon an ambulance arrived and loaded Jed into the back. Colin went over to the Sheriff, "Are you okay?"

"I am fine. You are a hero. You saved a life today. Thanks for your help."

"You're welcome. I should have said something earlier. Maybe this would not have happened."

"You did just fine. Go back to the diner and we can talk later."

Colin walked back to the diner and was greeted by Dan. "Wow, are you okay? We were watching everything from our windows."

Colin sat down and took a deep breath, "I am good. I am not sure about Jed. He was shot. One man was caught, the other was killed by the Sheriff."

Dan brought Colin a cup of coffee. "Sit for a while and collect your thoughts. Take off the apron, it has blood all over it."

Colin took off the apron and finished his coffee. After a short rest he returned to his job. What happened that afternoon was the talk of the town. Colin went about his job, ignoring the talk. He was worried about Jed. Soon Dan came to him.

"Why don't you call it a day. We can pick it up from here."

"Thanks, I would like to go check on Jed."

Colin went to his room and cleaned up. He walked out the door and made good time to the hospital. It is a small hospital, but it was a buzz with people running around talking about the shooting. When Colin walked to the front desk the woman recognized him.

"You are Colin. You want to see how Jed is doing."

"Yes, can you tell me what room he is in?"

"He is in surgery now. You can go to the nurse's station; they can give you more information."

Colin thanked the woman and walked to the nurse's station. He forgot all about Wil and his surgery. He asked the nurse if Jed was out of surgery, she said he was in recovery. "Can you tell me about Wil Wells?"

The nurse looked at her charts, "Yes, he is resting comfortably in his room."

Colin thanked the nurse and walked to Wil's room. "Hi there, young man."

Wil smiled as Colin walked into the room. Mary was sitting next to the bed and smiled too.

Mary stood, "I hear you are a hero."

Colin laughed, "I don't know why everybody thinks I am a hero. Didn't do anything."

"I heard you caught a bad guy and helped Jed."

Colin turned his attention to Wil. "How are you feeling?"

Wil smiled and said, "I feel great, but I am tired."

Mary responded, "the doctor said everything went very well. He said Wil should have a full recovery. It is the best Christmas present I could have ever had."

"Looks like we need to celebrate tonight." Colin stood up. "How about I fix you dinner tonight?"

Wil spoke up, "Yes, I think you should."

Mary smiled, "Okay, how about seven tonight?"

Colin gave Wil a high five and winked at Mary. "I will see you tonight."

Colin walked back to the Nurses station. "Can I see Jed?"

The Nurse said yes and pointed to his room.

Colin walked into Jed's room. Jed was very groggy but looked up when Colin entered.

"Hi Colin, how are you?"

"I am fine, how are you?"

"Doc says I will be just fine. I want to thank you for helping me. Doc said I could have died if you had not stopped the bleeding."

"I did what anybody would have done."

"I appreciate what you did for me. They say I will be home for Christmas."

"I will look forward to seeing you then."

Colin left the hospital and ran to the grocery store. He needed to pick up things for dinner. He was growing very fond of Mary, but he wasn't sure if she felt that way about him. After hitting the store, he noticed the lights at the Emporium. He walked into the Emporium and was greeted by Millie.

"Hi there Colin. I hear you had some excitement today. You saved Jed's life."

"Hi Mayor, I really wasn't a hero. I just helped Jed."

"Please call me Millie. I heard different. What can I do for you?"

"I am looking for something special for someone special."

Millie moved around the counter and walked to a jewelry case. "Here are some nice things for someone special."

Colin looked at the jewelry and picked a necklace. "I think this is the one."

"Nice choice, she will love this. I will put it in a nice gift box. Just give me a few minutes."

Colin walked around the room taking in all the amazing items. He came upon a Christmas display. It had a lodge and chair lifts going up a mountain. He thought this would be a nice thing to display during Christmas. "Hay Millie, how much for the Christmas town?"

"Oh, that is not for sale. It is a dream. I hoped to attract investors to build a ski resort. So far no investors."

"Why don't you have any investors? It seems like a great idea."

"Everyone who has looked at the plan says it will cost too much money. They don't believe we can attract enough people to make it payoff. I also included an upgrade of our Main Street. New light posts, new sidewalks, you know things to make out town look nice."

"What do you think it will cost?"

"Based on what investors say, it will cost close to one hundred million."

"Wow, that is a big investment."

"That is why we have no investors. It should pay for itself within two years." Millie completed wrapping the gift and handed it to Colin. Colin handed her the money for the purchase and thanked her for her help.

Colin raced from the Emporium to Mary's house. He immediately went to work on dinner. Mary was due soon. He put the wrapped gift under the tree so Mary could see it.

The front door opened and in walked Mary. "Oh, that smells good Colin."

"Are you hungry?"

"I am. What is for dinner?"

"Fried chicken and mashed potatoes and vegetables."

Mary went to the sink to wash her hands. "What is this?" She looked at the groceries on the counter.

"I just bought a few things I thought you might need."

Mary opened the refrigerator and saw it full of food. "You didn't need to do this."

"I wanted to make sure you and Wil had enough to eat when he comes home."

"Oh, Wil will be home tomorrow. The Doctor said he can go home, but he must take it easy. Thank you for this."

They sat down at the small kitchen table and quietly ate dinner. After dinner Colin moved to the small couch in the living room with two glasses and a bottle of wine. "Come sit down and relax. Have a glass of wine and enjoy."

Mary kicked off her shoes and sat on the couch. "I haven't been able to relax for some time. Now that Wil is safe and things are looking up, I can stop for a moment. I found out that all the hospital bills have been paid. No one at the hospital could tell me who did this. Now that I have a good car, I can breathe a little easier."

Colin poured a glass of wine for each of them and sat next to Mary. "I would be happy to help you with Wil. I can adjust my shift so I can be here when you are working. I like Wil a lot. He is a great kid."

"He sure loves you. He is always asking when you would be there. That would be great if you could help. I am not going back to work until after Christmas, so I can take care of Wil."

"How are you going to make ends meet?"

"Dan has said he will keep paying me until I come back."

"That is very nice."

"We won't have much of a Christmas because money will be tight for a while. I will just be happy to have Wil home."

The gift under the tree caught Mary's eye. "What is that?"

"It looks like a gift under the tree."

Mary walked to the tree and picked up the box. "Did you do this?"

"I couldn't resist. It just looked like you." Colin smiled.

Mary opened the box to find a beautiful gold charm neckless. The charm on it was a Christmas tree. "Oh my! This is beautiful. It must have cost you a lot of money."

"I don't have anybody to spend my money on, so you are the lucky recipient."

Mary sat back down on the couch and lifted her hair up. "Can you put this on please?"

Colin obliged and when he saw her milky white neck, he felt new emotions. He hooked the neckless on and Mary turned around.

"How does it look?"

"It looks beautiful, almost as beautiful as you."

Mary leaned over and kissed Colin on the lips. Colin returned the kiss. Mary leaned her head on his shoulder. "Tell me about your wife."

Colin took a deep breath, "Well she was my best friend. She was caring and giving. She could always see the best in people. I was always working, so I didn't give her all my attention. She was the light of my life. After she was gone, I knew I had lost the best thing that ever happened to me. I miss her so much."

Mary looked at Colin, "Why are you here?"

"I just could not stay where I was. There was no life in our house anymore. I was just wasting away. I needed to go out and see the good things in life. My wife would have wanted it this way. Now tell me about your husband."

Mary looked at Colin, "He was a good man. He made sure we were never in need of anything. He was my soul mate. He would walk into the room and just say I love you. Wil was his best friend. He will always be in my life."

Mary had a tear roll down her face. Colin reached over and wiped it off. Mary kissed his cheek. Mary stood up from the couch, "I need to get to the hospital early, so I think I should go to bed."

"Yes, it is late. I will come by tomorrow after work to check on you and Wil. Good night."

Mary walked him to the door and kissed his cheek again, "Thank you for dinner. Good night."

Colin walked down the street to his room smiling. He knew he was falling in love with Mary. He hasn't felt this way since he met his wife. He lay in his bed thinking of things to come.

Chapter 7

Colin woke the next morning and picked up his phone and dialed Williams. "Good morning, Williams. How is everything there?"

"Everything is fine here Sir. When might you be coming home?"

"Williams, I plan on being home Christmas Eve. I need to make sure the house is all decorated and we have the biggest Christmas Tree possible. I hope to have two guests for Christmas."

"Yes Sir. I will have the staff start right away."

"I will be sending you a list of things to be wrapped and placed under the tree. We will need to make dinner arrangements for us also. I will call you with more information when we get closer to Christmas."

"Yes Sir. I will look forward to hearing from you."

Collin hung up the phone and called his Attorney. "Glenn, this is Colin."

"Hi, Colin, where are you?"

"I am in a small town called Blue River. I love it here. I love the people here. You need to see this place. It is beautiful."

"I got a call from Williams; he told me you were on a mission."

"Yes, I decided that I needed to get out and quit feeling sorry for myself."

"Good for you. You needed to get out of your funk. What can I do for you?"

"I need you to investigate the information regarding a possible ski resort in Blue River. Several investors have investigated the possibility of building a resort here. I want to know why they decided not to invest."

"I will get right on it. When will I see you?"

"I will see you after Christmas. I don't want anybody to know it is me checking this out. You can make up a fake company, so they don't have any suspicions. I need to know as soon as possible."

"I will get right back to you."

"Text me and I will call you."

Colin hung up and got dressed for work. He walked from his room and into the back of the diner. He was immediately confronted by Dan.

"I just received the paperwork from your investor friend. Is this guy crazy?"

"What do you mean Dan?"

"Well, the paperwork is one page. It says there will be no payment on the note for five years. At the end of five years, it says if you are still in business, the loan will be forgiven. That means that if I stay in business for five years, I don't owe anything. There was a cashier's check attached for eight hundred thousand dollars."

Colin smiled, "Wow, I knew Bruce was a generous guy, but not like that."

Dan took a deep breath, "I am going to realize my dream. What a great Christmas present."

Colin sat and ate the breakfast Dan had prepared. Again, he thought that this is delicious. He finished and tied on his apron. He began to wash dishes left from the night before. He went about his job like usual and about an hour later the Sheriff came into the Diner.

"Good morning, Sheriff."

"Hi Colin, please call me Tom."

"Yes Sir."

Tom smiled and ordered a cup of coffee. "Colin, I need to talk to you about the General Store."

"Sure Sheriff, I mean Tom."

"I would like to have you meet me at the office tonight around six o'clock."

"Sure, what is this about?"

"I need to take your statement on the shooting. It should only take a few minutes."

"Okay, I will be there."

"Thanks Colin, I appreciate it."

The Sheriff finished his coffee and waived to Dan and walked out the door. Colin could hardly wait for his shift to be over, so he could see Mary and Wil.

As soon as his shift was over, he went to his room and changed. Out the door he dashed. He ran up the street and on to Mary's front porch. He knocked on the door. There was no response. He rang the doorbell and finally Mary answered.

"Hi Colin, come in. Sorry I didn't hear you at the door."

Colin walked into the apartment and was immediately hugged by Wil.

"Hey buddy, how are you feeling?"

Will looked up at Colin, "I feel much better now that I am home. Thank you for the Christmas tree!"

"You are welcome. I thought I saw a package under the tree for you."

"It's not Christmas yet."

"I don't know where it came from, it just appeared under the tree."

Wil moved to the box under the tree and began to unwrap the paper. "Wow, a jersey!"

"What kind of jersey?" Colin asked.

"It is a New York Rangers jersey, and it is autographed! Wait until I show this to my friends."

Mary looked at Colin and smiled. Colin rubbed Wil on the head and sat on the couch. Wil ran into his bedroom to try on the jersey.

"I know you did all of this." Mary walked over to the couch and sat next to him. "I can't thank you enough for this."

"After what Wil has been through, I think both of you needed some Christmas cheer."

Wil came out with his jersey on, "I don't think I will ever take this off!"

Colin and Mary smiled at Wil.

"I need to go to the Sheriff's Office at six tonight. Would you like to go to dinner after?"

Mary had a sheepish smile on her face, "How about if we drive you there and wait?"

"I don't know how long I will be."

"We will be okay. Let's go."

They all got into Mary's new car. Wil asked, "Mom when did you get this car?"

"I won it a few days ago. Can you believe this?"

Wil smiled, "It's the Christmas Angel. I have been praying for help."

Colin smiled, "It is super nice. You guys will travel in style now."

Mary started the car and they drove off down the street. Soon they arrived at the Sheriff's Office.

Colin jumped out, "Wil do you want to come with me? You can see the inside of the Sheriff's Office."

"Can I go mom?"

"Sure, but you take it easy. I will go park the car."

Colin and Wil walked into the Office. There was a woman at the desk. Colin walked up to the desk.

"Hi, I am Colin Wade. I am here to see the Sheriff."

"Oh, yes. He is expecting you. Just walk down the hall and through the doors. You will see him."

The two walked down the hall and opened the doors. Suddenly, they were met with a loud applause. Colin stopped in his tracks and looked around at everybody in the room. They kept applauding and Colin just stood there. He thought there must be some mistake. It's not my birthday. Mayor Taylor stepped out of the crowd and grabbed his hand. She led him to an area near the podium.

"Attention everyone, this is Colin Wade. He saved our friend Jed Johnson. He also assisted in capturing one of the robbers. Colin we would all like to thank you for being part of our community. We would like to give you this token of our appreciation. The Key to Our Hearts." Milly handed Colin a small box with a gold key.

Colin still couldn't believe what was happening. He looked at the crowd and smiled. Sheriff Daily stepped up to the podium.

"As Sheriff of Blue River, I would like to award Colin with an honorary position of Deputy with our department." He handed Colin a Sheriff's badge and shook his hand.

Colin was dumbfounded, he just stood there. Mayor Taylor grabbed his arm and pulled him to the podium. "I don't know what to say except Thank You. I only did what I believe most of you would have done. I am proud to be a member of this community. I believe many good things are going to make this an outstanding place to live. Thank you all."

Mayor Taylor stepped up to the podium, "Okay everyone there are refreshments and snacks on the tables behind you. Let's have some fun."

The crowd descended on Colin shaking his hand and patting him on the back. Soon Jed stepped up to Colin.

"I want to thank you for being there for me. I would have bled to death if it wasn't for you. Oh, one more thing." Jed handed Colin a piece of paper.

"What is this?"

"Open it."

Colin opened the small piece of paper. It was a bill for one tee shirt. "Colin began to laugh."

The crowd all began to laugh. Colin looked around the room and saw Mary and Wil standing by the food tables. He walked over to the two. "I have a feeling you knew about this."

Mary and Will laughed, "Well we couldn't tell you anything about this."

"Wil I can't believe you let them do this to me." Colin smiled at Wil. Wil hugged Colin and gave him a big smile.

After a half hour the mayor announced that it was time for the snowman contest. Everybody moved out of the room to the town square and lined up for the contest. There were about two hundred people there wanting to see the festivities.

Wil looked at Colin, "Can we do this?"

"I don't know if it would be good for you right now. Remember the Doctor said to take it easy."

Mary looked at Wil, "No, you can watch, you will not be building a snowman."

Wil looked down at the ground, "Okay."

Colin spoke up, "How about if your mom and I build one. You can tell us what to do."

Wil grinned, "Okay!"

Mary tugged at Colin's arm as if to say what are you doing. Colin led Mary to the area where the snowmen were being built and they began to work on building a snowperson. After a half hour it was taking shape. Wil brought over some branches for the arms and three stones for eyes and nose.

Colin stepped back and looked at the almost finished snowman, "Wil what else does it need?"

Wil looked at the snowman and said, "Wait a minute I will be right back."

Mary watched Wil walk toward the skating rink. "What do you think he is up to?"

"I don't know. Maybe he has decided not to do this."

Colin looked at Mary and stepped close to her, "This is the best Christmas I have had in a long time."

"Me too," Mary replied.

Colin leaned over and kissed Mary on the lips. Mary responded by pulling Colin's head down to her. They stood looking at each other for a few seconds.

"I didn't think I could have these feelings for anyone again. You have brought those feelings back to me. Thank you."

Mary looked up at him, "I feel the same way about you. I feel love again."

Colin placed his arm around Mary's shoulders, she rested her head on his chest. Wil was now walking toward them. When he saw his mother with Colin he smiled and felt happy.

"Look what I have," Wil shouted.

Wil had a hockey stick and hockey pads. "We can put these on the snowman and make him a hockey player!"

Colin lifted the head off the snowman and Wil placed the shoulder pads on. He placed two leg pads at the base of the snowman and then the hockey stick in his hand.

"Now he looks like a hockey player!"

Mary and Colin stepped back and looked at the hockey man.

"I think he looks great!" Colin responded. "Now we need to wait for the judges to come by. Let's go get some hot chocolate."

They walked over to the booth with the hot chocolate and Colin and Mary held hands. Soon it was time for the judge's announcement. Everybody moved to the podium area and began to mill around.

"Okay, ladies and gentlemen, it is that time, time for the announcement of the winners. Mayor Taylor will announce the winners."

The mayor moved to the podium, "All right, here we go. I need to say, this year we had some great snowmen. So, for the third-place winner, the Ed Parker family." They walked to the podium and received their trophy. "The second-place winner is Wil Wells." Mary jumped up and down.

"Wil get up there and accept the trophy!" Mary pushed Wil toward the podium.

Colin clapped and whistled while Wil walked to the podium. Wil got the trophy and walked back his mom.

"Wow, I guess it is not bad for someone who had not planned to enter the contest." Mary said.

Wil was happy and had a big smile on his face. Colin put his arm on Wil's shoulder, "Let's go home. I think we have all had enough excitement for one day." They walked back to Mary's car and Mary dropped Colin off at his room.

"Thank you all for tonight. I had a wonderful time. Will I see you tomorrow?"

Wil pipped up, "Please come over. We can watch the hockey game together."

"Okay, I will see you tomorrow." Colin waved as they drove off.

Colin walked into his room and sat on the bed. Wow, he thought. I didn't think I would be falling in love. He checked his phone, there was a message from his attorney Glenn Davis. It was too late to call him now, so it will need to wait until morning. Colin went to bed with visions of Mary dancing in his head.

Chapter 8

Colin walked into the diner as he always did every morning, Dan was smiling at him. "Why are you smiling at me?"

"I just can't forget your face last night when you walked into the room. We got you. I have never seen you smile like that. Now sit down and eat your breakfast."

Colin smiled and ate his breakfast. He tied his apron on and went to work. He cleaned tables and wiped off the counter. He brought all the clean glasses from the dishwasher. People coming into the diner would shake his hand and thank him for what he did. This went on most of the day. Finally, Colin got his first break. He went to his room and called Glenn.

"Hi Glenn."

"Hi Colin, I have the information you asked for. I contacted two of my friends in the business and they both had the same opinion."

"What was their opinion?"

"Well, they believe it was too much money to accomplish what the town wanted. They didn't say it was a risky investment. They said it can work, it just was too expensive."

"Okay, please contact Donald at Wade Construction and let him know that after the holidays I will need his full attention on this project. I will be funding the project."

"Are you sure you want to do this?"

"I am sure. I love this town and I want it to be successful. I will need you to call Mayor Taylor and let her know that an investor wants to move forward with her project. Let her know that after the holidays the investor and a contractor would like to meet with her regarding the start of this project."

"If she asks about the investor?"

"Just say he will meet her after the holiday."

"Okay, I will handle this for you. Can you tell me what you are doing there?"

"I am finding my life again."

"Okay, I am glad, you have been silent for too long. I will text you with any information you need to know. If I don't talk to you before then, Merry Christmas."

"Merry Christmas to you and your wife. There will be a bonus for you under the tree this year."

"Thanks Colin."

Colin hung up the phone and took a deep breath, I think Lynn would be happy and proud about what I am doing. Okay, back to work.

Colin went about his job with a smile. He could hardly wait to see Mary and Wil that afternoon. A young woman came into the diner and asked for Dan. Dan came out and greeted the woman with a hug. He sat her down in an empty booth and they began to talk. Colin came over to the booth.

"Can I get you a cup of coffee?"

Dan looked at Colin, "Oh, Colin this is Jennifer she is our Christmas charity organizer. She is here to hand out donation envelopes."

"Christmas envelopes?"

"Yes, she does this every year. She asks that people place money in the envelopes and deposit them in a box in City Hall. The money will go to buy Christmas for needy families in town."

"Wow, that is great. How many families will this benefit?"

Jennifer looked at Colin, "This year we have forty families who need help. The money will buy Christmas food and toys for each family. It always depends on how much we collect if we are going to have a good Christmas or just a fair Christmas."

Colin asked, "How much money is a good Christmas?"

"We collected two thousand last year and that was good."

Colin smiled, "I will take an envelope. I don't have much, but I will give what I can."

Jennifer handed him an envelope and thanked him. Colin went back to work and now he had another cause to help with. Soon, it was time to change and go to Mary's. Colin retrieved his phone and dialed Williams.

"Williams, I need another favor."

"Yes sir, what can I do."

"I have run out of cash. I need you to go to the safe and get ten thousand out. Place it in a large envelope and bring it to me here. Meet me down the street from the diner at two tomorrow. Can you do that?"

"Yes sir, I will be there at two. Is there anything else?"

"No, that should be good. How is the Christmas decorating coming?"

"You will love it sir. All the gifts you requested are under the exceptionally large tree. Outside is beautiful. The decorators finished yesterday. It looks just like it did when Mrs. Wade coordinated it."

"Thanks Williams, I don't know what I would do without you. I will see you tomorrow."

"Yes sir, I will see you then."

Colin changed and headed out the door to Mary's.

Wil answered the door and gave Colin a big hug. "I am glad you are here. Mom said we can go see Santa tonight."

"Wow, Santa. Where is he going to be?"

"He will be at the town square."

Mary walked into the room. "I guess he has told you about Santa. He is extremely excited to give him his Christmas list."

"Well, I wonder if I can give him my Christmas list?"

Mary laughed, "I am sure he will take your list."

Wil was even more excited, "Can we go now?"

Colin laughed, "Well I guess we can. What about it mom?"

"Santa will not be there until five tonight. We have a short time to wait."

Colin piped up, "I have an idea. I would like to take a drive to see where Mayor Millie wants to build this ski resort she was talking about."

Mary nodded her head, "We can do that. Wil go get your jacket and cap on then we can go."

They jumped into Mary's car and drove out of town into a heavily wooded area. Mary parked the car in a turnout. "Here it is. This is the area. You can look up there and see where the ski slopes would be. The town owns all the area up those mountains and all the property below them. They were given to the town by the man who settled this area and founded the town."

Colin looked at the mountains and the forest area. "Wow, this is beautiful. I can see a lodge and ski resort here."

"Yes, and I know that the mayor wants this to be as little impact on the forest as possible. She said she wants to preserve as much of the forest as possible. No tree clearing except for what is absolutely necessary."

"That is great. I think this will be a big success. I wonder why no company wants to invest?"

"I don't know. The mayor has been working on this for a long time, she has the whole community behind her. If it is successful, she says she will be able to cut property taxes and fully fund our schools."

Colin shook his head in approval. "I hope someone will take on this project."

Wil yelled, "Can we go now!"

Mary and Colin smiled. They went back to the car and headed back to town. The town square was busy with people and Christmas music echoed through the square. Last night's snow covered the ground. Wil jumped out of the car and made his way to the area where Santa was sitting. Mary and Colin followed Wil to Santa's throne.

"Mary, do you know what is on his Christmas list?"

"Yes, I don't know how to tell him that Santa may only be able to bring one thing this year. I am living on waitress pay. I am so grateful that the hospital bill was paid. I am just making ends meet. I still don't know who paid that bill, but I am grateful."

Colin wrapped his arm around Mary and pulled her close to him. "You know you need to pray for the Christmas Angel. Wil did and see what happened for him."

Mary laughed, "Maybe I will."

Colin and Mary walked closer to watch Wil with Santa. Wil sat in Santa's lap and had a big smile on his face. He handed Santa a paper with his list. Santa smiled and tucked the paper in his coat. He handed Wil a large candy cane. Wil jumped off his lap and ran to his mom.

"Well, how did that go?"

"He said he would see what he could do."

Colin laughed, "Okay, what do you say we go get something to eat?"

Wil shouted, "I am hungry!"

The local Mexican restaurant was the next stop.

Dinner was excellent and they were all pleasantly full. The ride home was quiet because they all were Christmas happy. They drove up the driveway to Mary's apartment and piled out of the car.

"It is so festive here. Now that you decorated the place. Wil loves it. He can't wait to turn the outside lights on every night," Mary stated.

Colin motioned to Wil, "Come here Wil." Wil stood next to Colin. "So, what did you ask Santa for?"

"Well, I gave him my list."

"What would be your number one gift you asked for?"

"I asked for tickets to a Rangers game."

"Oh, tickets, I see. The Rangers. How would you get there?"

"Mom will drive me. Right mom?"

Mary chuckled, "I guess I will. It is time for bed."

Reluctantly, Will vanished to the bedroom. Soon he was back with his pajamas on.

"Did you brush your teeth?" Mary asked.

"Yes, mom. All done. Good night Colin."

"Good night my little man. See you tomorrow."

Colin looked at the door, "I guess I better get going."

Mary stood up from the couch, "Stay a little longer. I haven't had a conversation with another man for a long time. I would sit with my husband; we would talk about our future. I enjoyed our conversations."

"I would love to stay a while. I miss conversations with my wife. First, I need to tell you something."

Mary looked at Colin. "What?"

"I have strong feelings for you. I think I am falling in love with you. I didn't think I could ever feel this way again. I am a lucky to have fallen in love twice. I hope I am not being too forward."

Mary moved closer to Colin, "I feel the same way. I felt something different when I first saw you in the diner. I must think of Wil when I meet someone. I don't want him to be hurt. He really likes you. I do too."

Colin pulled Mary to him then passionately kissed her. She kissed him back and leaned over to place her head on his chest. They kissed and hugged for quite some time and became entangled in each other's bodies.

Colin stopped and looked at Mary, "I think I should go. I don't want to wake Wil."

Mary stood up, "I know, I forget this is a small place and he can hear everything."

Colin moved to the door and Mary followed, kissing him as he opened the door. Colin gave her a hug and kissed her again. "I will see you tomorrow."

Colin walked down the steps and back to his room. He hoped she would still love him after she found out who he was. He checked his messages, there were no messages. He laid on his bed and smiled. He was happy again. He had forgotten what it was like to be in love.

Chapter 9

Colin woke and dressed as usual. He looked out the one window and saw fresh snow on the ground. He began to sing It's Beginning to Look a Lot Like Christmas. Not knowing all the words, he began to whistle. He entered the diner and put on his apron. Dan had prepared him a gourmet breakfast as usual. Everyone was busy getting ready to open. Colin finished his food and finished cleaning the dishes from last night. The waitresses were busy filling salt, pepper, sugar. Everyone seemed to be in a great mood.

Colin started to wipe off tables in the back of the diner. "Thanks Colin. I appreciate your help." Laura said, as she filled a sugar canister. Colin smiled.

The day went by quickly and he was excited to see Williams. He hung up his apron and said goodbye to the staff and went to his room to clean up. He grabbed the envelope for the Christmas charity and exited his room. The snow was about three inches deep and made his progress terribly slow. He looked down the street and could see a limousine parked next to an empty lot. As Colin approached the side door opened. Colin looked around to make sure no one was watching then stepped into the car.

"Hi Williams, it is good to see you."

"It is exceptionally good to see you sir. Have you been all right?"

"I feel the best I have felt in many years. I have fallen in love, Williams."

"You have sir?"

"I met a beautiful woman here and she has brought life back to me. Her name is Mary, she has a young son Wil. Wil was the one in the hospital and why I needed you to call Dr. Jacobs."

"Is the young man doing well?"

"Dr. Jacobs made him as good as new. He is a great little boy. You will like him."

"I have the money you asked for." Williams produced an envelope full of cash.

Colin took five thousand out of the envelope and placed it in the charity envelope. "I need you to drop this off. You must be a little stealth and make sure you don't attract attention to you. I don't want anybody to know where this came from. There is a box in City Hall marked for Christmas Charity. Drop it off there and leave."

Williams nodded his head and placed the envelope in his coat pocket.

"If all goes well Williams, I plan on having Wil and Mary to the house for Christmas Eve. That is why I asked you to get everything decorated. I will be texting you with some of the things I want you to get for under the tree. I want this to be a magical Christmas for all of us."

"Yes sir, I will do my best. How are you going to get them here?"

"I am not sure yet. I will call or text you with the plans."

"Yes sir, I will wait for you to let me know. I will have everything ready."

Colin placed the remaining money in his jacket and stepped out of the car. He looked around again and felt sure no one had seen him. The limo started and went up the street to the City Hall. Colin heard a car pull up behind him. It was Sheriff Daily.

"Hi Colin, how are you?"

"Hi Sheriff, I am fine. How are you?"

"I am good, do you have a minute?"

"Sure, what is up?"

"Well, after the shooting, I had to do checks on everybody involved. I didn't find anything for your name. So, I googled your name. Well, you are Colin Wade of Wade investment and Money Management. You are a Billionaire."

Colin smiled, "Well not all true. I was the CEO of that company, but I retired a few years ago."

The Sheriff laughed, "So tell me what you are doing here."

"I will tell you if you promise me that you will keep this between us."

"Well, I guess I can keep a secret. What is the story?"

Colin opened the patrol car door and sat in the passenger seat. "I lost my wife to a car accident a few years ago. After the accident I went into a shell. I didn't leave the house and I fell into deep depression. Recently, I was watching a program on TV and realized I needed to find a way out of this funk. The program showed people who needed help to make their lives easier. I thought I could do that. My wife was always working with charities and helping those in need. I believed I could do the same. I decided to just wander, looking like someone who needed help himself. That is how I found my way here."

"That explains the new MRI machine at the hospital and the world-famous doctor who just happened to show up to fix Wil. I assume you are behind Dan getting his loan for a new restaurant and Mary's hospital bills going away. So, what is next?"

"You will just need to wait and see. I do believe the mayor's wish to have a ski resort may be coming true."

"Oh good! Maybe I will get some much-needed equipment. We will need to expand the department. That will be great. This town needs some cash. We are small and don't always have the money to buy the things we need. I have not had a new patrol car for five years. All six of my patrol cars have over two hundred thousand miles on them. Now the Mayor will have no excuse to not give the department what we need. That is good news!"

"Remember, you know nothing about any of this."

"My lips are sealed. Just let me know if you need anything."

"I will. Thanks for being discrete."

Colin jumped out of the patrol car and waived as Sheriff Daily drove off. He pulled his phone out of his pocket and dialed a number. "Hi, this is Colin Wade I need to speak to Rick."

Soon a voice on the phone, "Hey Colin, how have you been?"

"I am good. How is business?"

"It could be better, but we are doing good. What can I do for you?"

"Do you still have a friend who preps cars for police departments?"

"Yes, he does just about all the departments around here. Why?"

"I want seven SUVs delivered to your friend to be set up for the Blue River Police Department."

"Seven SUV's?"

"Yes, I want you to deliver the SUVs to your friend. I want them to be the best you have. Four-wheel drive and all the bells and whistles. When they are complete, please deliver them to Sheriff Daily at the Blue River police department."

"Well, I told you business was good, it just got exceptionally good. How was the other SUV we delivered to you?"

"It was perfect. Just send the bill to my Attorney Glenn Davis. He will take care of all of it. Merry Christmas!"

"Merry Christmas to you. It will be a Merry Christmas."

"Thanks Rick, I will be talking to you soon."

Colin hung up and returned his phone to his pocket. He was anxious to get to Mary's house. He walked quickly to her house. Wil was waiting on the porch.

"Hi Colin. What took you? I have been waiting."

"I came as soon as I could."

Wil handed Colin a hockey stick. "Will you play a little hockey with me?"

"Sure! It has been some time since I played hockey, but I will give it a try."

Wil grabbed his stick; they went to the street to hit the puck around. Soon Mary came out and sat on the front steps watching the two playing hockey. Wil and Colin played for about a half hour when Mary stood up.

"Okay, time to cool it for a while. Time to rest for a while."

"Oh mom, do we have to? We are having fun."

Colin put his hand on Wil's shoulder. "I think we should stop for now."

The two went into the house and Wil opened the refrigerator, pulling out a bottle of sports drink. "That was fun. Thanks Colin."

"You are welcome. Maybe when the doctor gives you clearance we can play longer."

Mary walked out of the kitchen, "Okay, we are going to the town square for Christmas carols. Everybody, get your jackets and hats."

"Okay, you know I can't sing." Colin chuckled.

"It doesn't matter we are all going to the square."

They all went out, piled into Mary's SUV, drove to the square.

The square was filled with people carrying candles and gathering near the stage. A man was handing out song books and singing. Everybody was in a Christmas mood, shaking hands and hugging. Soon, the music started, Wil grabbed Colins hand and dragged him toward the stage. Mary followed smiling at the newfound friendship. After an hour of Christmas carols, the mayor stepped up to the microphone, "Great news about this year's Christmas charity. We have exceeded last year's donations. We had an anonymous donation of five thousand dollars. We will be able to provide a wonderful Christmas to all those in need this year." Sheriff Daily turned and looked at Colin, then smiled.

Colin turned to Mary, "I need to get a present for my nephew. He is about the same age as Wil, where can we go?"

"We can go to the mall, it's small but there are stores there that will have anything you might need."

Off to the car and to the mall. Wil smiled, "Can we go to the toy store?"

Colin laughed, "Of course we can. You can pick out some toys my nephew might like."

Wil jumped out of the car as soon as they parked at the mall. He was excited to get into the store and see all the toys.

Mary became concerned, "Wil, calm down. I don't want you to get too tired."

"Okay mom, can you hurry, we need to get in there before all the toys are gone!"

Colin laughed, "I have a feeling that there will be plenty of toys to go around."

Colin picked up Mary's hand as they walked into the mall. Mary looked at Colin and smiled. They walked into the first store and Mary quietly looked at a beautiful black dress on a mannequin. Colin kept watching, then walked over to her.

"Nice dress, it would look good on you."

"Have you looked at the price tag?"

"It can't be that much. Wow! I guess I haven't bought a dress lately."

Mary laughed, "I would need to work a whole lot of overtime to afford this."

Wil yelled, "Mom come on, over here!"

Wil was over in the toy area and had an excited look. Mary and Colin walked over to the toy department where the excited Wil was hovering.

"Over here! This is the bike I think your nephew would like."

Colin walked over to the bicycle and looked. "This is really nice; do you have one like this?"

"Oh no, I don't have a bike. Since I was sick, I couldn't ride one."

Colin looked at Mary, "I think my nephew would love this."

Colin looked at Wil, "Are you okay? You look tired."

Wil slumped to the floor; Mary screamed. Colin grabbed Wil and picked him up.

"Let's go. You drive to the hospital!"

Colin carried Wil to the car and sat in the back seat with Wil. Mary started the car and hurried to the hospital. They drove to the emergency entrance. Colin carried Wil into the room where two nurses took Wil. Mary followed Wil to a room. Colin walked outside and made a call.

"Can I speak to Dr. Jacobs please? Tell him it is Colin Wade."

"Well, I didn't think I would be hearing from you this soon."

"The boy is back in the hospital. He passed out while we were shopping. I took him to the emergency room."

"I will call the Doctor there and see what is going on. Don't worry, I am sure he will be all right."

Colin hung up the phone and walked back into the hospital. Mary was sitting in the waiting room with her head in her hands.

Colin was concerned, "What is wrong?"

Mary looked up at Colin, "I needed to pay more attention to Wil. I got off track. I can't be with you. I need to make sure Wil is taken care of. I like you very much, but right now I need to focus on Wil."

Mary stood up and kissed Colin on the cheek and walked back into the emergency room. Colin could not believe what just happened. He hung his head and walked out of the hospital. He had fallen in love with Mary and loved Wil. He walked down the street and caught the attention of Mayor Millie.

"Hi Colin."

"Hi Mayor."

"What is the long face for?"

"Well, it is a long story."

"I have plenty of time and I have some fresh coffee. Come on in, I was just about to close up."

Colin walked up the steps to the Emporium. Millie opened the door and they both walked into the store. Millie locked the door behind them.

"Colin come back to my office."

"Nice office!" Colin exclaimed.

"Follow me." Millie walked up a flight of stairs into a nicely decorated room. "This is my home. I live above the store. As a matter of fact, I own the entire block."

Colin stood looking around the living room. "I love all the antiques. These are beautiful. I assume you are a collector?"

"Well, I started when my husband was still alive. One thing here another there, soon I had a house full. When my husband died, I sold everything and bought the real estate. I decided to open the emporium to keep me busy."

"Wow, this is nice. How do you like living above the store?"

"I love it. I can take a break and come up here and make some coffee. So, sit and I will get us some coffee."

Colin sat on the beautiful antique couch. He looked at a picture on the mantle. "Is the photo on the mantle your husband?"

"Yes, that was taken about a year before he died."

Millie returned with two cups of coffee, "Okay tell me your long story."

"Well, as you may know Mary Wells and I have been seeing each other for the last two weeks. I have become attached to Wil. Everything was going well until tonight."

"What happened?"

"We went shopping at the mall and Wil got sick and passed out."

"Oh no! Is he alright?"

"I don't know. He was still in the emergency room when I left."

"Why did you leave?"

"Mary decided I should go because she was paying too much attention to me, not paying attention to Wil."

"Colin, you know that was emotion talking. She is so worried about Wil that she could not think right."

"I hope that is all it is. I have fallen in love with her. I love Wil as if he were mine. I know that I am just a working stiff. I don't make much money, but I will do whatever I need to do to take care of them."

"I would just give her a little space and she will come around. When Wil is out of the hospital, she will be fine."

Chapter 10

Colin walked out of the Emporium and walked through the park. He noticed the lights on an old Victorian house across the park. He wanted a closer look at the mansion. It was beautiful. As he got closer, he noticed a young boy sitting at the bottom of the steps to the house. The boy looked sad.

"Hi there young man. What are you doing sitting out here in the dark and cold?"

The boy looked at Colin, "I am just thinking."

"Boy, you are thinking hard. I can see the smoke coming out of your ears."

The boy felt his ears, "Smoke?"

Colin laughed and said, "Just kidding. What are you so deep in thought about?"

"Just wondering if I will ever be adopted."

Colin sat next to the boy, "Why do you think that?"

"I have been here for two years, no one wants me."

"You live here? It looks like a nice place to live."

"I guess it is okay. It's not like living in a house with a family. My mom and dad were killed in a car accident two years ago. I just want to be a family again."

"So, this is an orphanage?"

"Yes sir. Christmas makes it hard. My parents always made Christmas special. Lights, a big tree, lots of presents and Christmas music."

"Don't you have a tree here?"

"There is a small tree on a table in the living room. I think that it is all we can afford. We usually get one gift, it is clothes. I just miss my mom and dad. What about you?"

"Well, I am just visiting here for a short time. My wife died in a car accident, so I just don't know how to celebrate without her."

"Sounds like me. Just not the same."

"Let's go in the house where it is warm, okay?"

The boy got up and walked up the long stairs to the front door. He opened the door; an older woman was standing there. "Where have you been Ben?" She looked at Colin.

"Hi, I am Colin and I found him sitting on the steps deep in thought."

"I am Susan, this is my home. I have been fostering children for ten years."

"The house is beautiful."

"It has been in my family for one hundred years. It needs a little TLC. I don't have the money to really fix it up. I don't get much money from the State, but we make do. Would you like a tour?"

Colin smiled, "Yes, I would love that."

Susan walked Colin through the house. It was a little sparce. There were no gifts under the small Christmas tree. The dining room table was set for dinner and there were ten place settings. It had a large kitchen with room to do the cooking for ten children. Up the stairs to the bedrooms. There were six bedrooms, one of them was Susan's. Three bathrooms that needed some work. The rooms were set up for the five boys and five girls. The older girls and boys had rooms and the younger children were split between the remaining rooms. The bunk beds were old and needed to be replaced. All the beds needed to be replaced.

Susan was right, there was a lot of work to be done. Colin looked at the children playing in the living room. They all seemed happy. The toys they had were old and very used.

"The house is genuinely nice. You have used your space well, Collin said as he walked into the foyer. Can I have the names and ages of the children. I would like to buy them a Christmas present."

Susan smiled, "I would be happy to give you that. We don't have much money to buy gifts for them."

"Don't you get any of the gifts from the town Christmas donations?"

"No, since we get money from the State, they don't see us as needy."

Colin shook his head, "That is too bad. I will make sure you get some gifts. Tell me about young Ben."

"Yes, Ben is an exceptionally good child. He had some trouble adjusting after his parents' death. He has come out of his shell and is making the best of things."

Susan walked into the little office next to the foyer. Soon she returned with the list Colin requested.

Colin walked to the door and thanked Susan for the tour. He turned to the children, "Hey Ben, it was nice talking to you." Ben smiled and waved at Colin.

Colin walked down the long steps to the sidewalk and walked back to his room. He knew what he needed to do. It was only eight o'clock, so he called Williams.

Williams answered the phone, "Yes, Mr. C, how are you and how can I help?"

"I am fine Williams. I have another project for you. Get a pencil and paper."

"Yes sir, at your service."

Colin read off all the names and ages of the children at the foster home. "I know we only have a few days to Christmas, but I know between you and Kathy this will get done. I want four or five gifts for each child. They are to be delivered to Ms. Susan at the foster home. Have Glenn Include a check to her for fifty thousand to help with operating expenses. Have Glenn contact my contractor and have him evaluate the needs to get the house in good order. Let him know that whatever the cost, I will cover it."

"Is that all sir?"

"One more thing, have Glenn's legal team look into what it would take to adopt one of the children."

"Yes sir, adopt?"

"Williams, I am interested in a young man named Ben. He seems to be a wonderful boy."

"Yes, I will make sure Glenn gets on it."

"Thanks Williams, I will be in contact with you soon." Colin hung up his phone and tucked it in its hiding place, then laid back on the bed.

Colin woke to the smell of Dan's breakfast special. He bathed and shaved then dawned his work clothes. He walked in the back door of the diner and was met by Dan.

"Good morning!" Dan said as Colin walked into the back room.

"Good morning," Colin replied.

Dan walked over to Colin. "What is up?"

"Well, Wil had a relapse last night."

"I spoke to Mary this morning she told me Wil was just fine."

Colin looked at Dan. "She said he is okay?"

"Yes, and she asked if you were here. I told her you were not in yet. You need to call her."

Colin smiled, "I guess I better call her."

Dan pointed to the door, "Give her a call."

Colin walked out the back door and retrieved his cell phone from his room. He dialed her number.

"Hello Colin," the voice said.

"Hello Mary."

"Colin, I am sorry for what I said last night. I was so concerned about Wil; I could not think about anything else."

Colin took a deep breath, "I was very worried about Wil, I was not thinking about your feelings."

Mary was quiet on the phone, "I think I am falling in love with you."

"I know I am in love with you," Colin added.

"Wil is extremely attached to you. The first thing he asked me was where is Colin?"

"I love that little boy. I can't imagine not having him around."

Mary looked back at Wil who was listing to the conversation. "We would love it if

you could come over tonight for dinner."

"I would love to." Colin responded.

Colin walked back into the restaurant and was greeted by Dan. "Well, did you get it fixed?"

Colin smiled, "Yes I think so."

Dan smiled, "I think you need to take the day off."

"I can't do that to you."

"Oh, it is okay. I want to introduce you to Scott; he is our new dishwasher."

"Does that mean I am out of a job?"

"No, I am promoting you to server."

"Well, that is nice, but I was going to tell you, I will be moving on the week before Christmas."

"You can't leave now. This town has adopted you. You are a big part of this town."

Colin sat at the table, "I understand, but I have some unfinished business elsewhere."

Dan nodded his head, "You will be back?"

"I love this town. I will be back."

Chapter 11

Colin went to work cleaning tables and washing dishes. He showed the new dishwasher the ropes. He knew he would be leaving in a day or two. Should he tell Mary? Should he keep quiet until Christmas? He will tell Mary tonight that he is leaving for a day or two tomorrow. He needs to take care of business at home. He wants to see about getting the little boy Ben from the orphanage. He would like to have him home for Christmas. He will go to the orphanage tonight and talk to Susan the owner to see what he needs to do to get Ben.

Colin finished the last of the day's dishes. Dan walked into the back, "Okay, it's time to go. Spend some time with Mary. Tell her we miss her."

"Thanks Dan, I will tell her."

Colin went to his room and cleaned up. He checked his phone, but there were no messages. Off he went to the orphanage. The big house was just up the road, and he could see the beautiful spires of the old house. He took a big breath before walking up the steps to the front door. Susan answered the door.

"Hello Colin, come in."

"Thank you, Susan."

"What can I do for you?"

"Well, I would like to talk to you about Ben."

Susan led Colin to her office. "Have a seat. So, you were impressed with our little Ben."

Colin smiled, "Our little conversation the other night on the front steps won me over. I am sure there are other kids here who would love to have an opportunity to get adopted, but I fell in love with Ben."

"I got a call from social services; they told me there was someone interested in adopting Ben. I knew who it was, so I contacted the Sheriff. Sheriff Daily said I would be a fool if I didn't let Ben go with you for Christmas. He said you are a good man."

"That was nice of him. I like Ben a lot and I want to give him a nice Christmas."

"Where are you going to take him?"

"I have a home about an hour from here and I have invited a few friends to be there."

"If you don't mind me asking, why are you doing dishes and living in Dan's back room?"

"When my wife died, I was in a funk and decided to travel for a while. I stumbled on to this town and fell in love with all the people here. I plan on finding a place to stay here after the holidays."

Susan smiled, "This is a great place to live. I have lived here all my life. I thought I might lose this house a few years back, but the State came up with more money to keep me going."

Colin looked around her office, "You need more room."

"If I had the money, I wanted to build office space on the back of the house. We could use this room for another bedroom."

"You never know, maybe Santa will put some money in your stocking." Colin smiled and walked out of the room.

Susan laughed, "I won't hold my breath."

Ben was sitting on the floor playing with some Legos, Colin walked over and sat on the floor next to him. "What are you building?"

"I am building a house."

Colin shook his head, "I like building things. Maybe we can build something together."

Ben smiled and shoved some blocks toward Colin. The two spent an hour talking and building a house.

"Hey Ben, I need to go, but would you like to come to my house for Christmas?"

Ben's eyes got big, "Do you have a Christmas tree?"

"Yes, a big one. Maybe Santa will bring us some blocks to build a house."

Ben jumped up and hugged Colin. "I can't wait!"

"I will pick you up soon, so you need to be good until then."

"Yes sir!"

Colin thanked Susan and walked to the door, waiving to Ben. As he walked down the steps to the house, he smiled. His wife would have been excited and happy. He walked down the street toward Mary's apartment, soon he was at the door. Before he could knock, Wil swung the door open and hugged Colin.

"Hey there little man. Good to see you are feeling better."

"The doctor said I had just over did it."

"Well, we need to take it easy for a few days." Colin looked up at Mary as she walked to the door.

Mary smiled at Colin, "I am so sorry. I was so scared."

Colin reached out and pulled Mary to him, "I understand."

Colin walked into the apartment and Wil closed the door.

Wil asked, "Where have you been? I expected you earlier."

"Do you know where the orphanage is?" Colin asked.

"Yes, I have some friends there." Wil said.

"Well, there is a boy there named Ben. I was visiting him."

Wil smiled, "I know Ben. We play together all the time. He is my friend. I think we are about the same age. I like him a lot."

Colin looked at Mary, "I was playing Legos with him. I was thinking about inviting him to share Christmas with us. Would that be okay you and your mom?"

Mary smiled, "I think that would be a wonderful idea."

Wil jumped up, "I could show him my room and we can play some games!"

Colin walked over to Mary and hugged her. "I need to talk to you about Christmas."

Mary looked concerned, "Is everything all right?"

"Everything is good, I have a few gifts for you and Wil I have a surprise for you both."

Wil's ears perked up, "Surprise?"

Mary laughed, "Why don't you go play with your tablet and let Colin and I talk."

Wil moved to his room, Mary and Colin sat on the small couch in the living room.

"I need to let you know that I am leaving town for a few days."

"Where are you going," Mary asked.

"I need to attend to business out of town."

Mary looked at Colin, "You have business out of town? You are a dishwasher at a restaurant."

"I know, before I came here, I left some unfinished business at my old home. I have been on the road for some time, I do have to make sure everything is okay at home. I will make sure we are all together for Christmas. I would love to have you visit my house someday."

Mary leaned her head on Colin's shoulder, "I would love to know more about your life."

"I promise you we will talk at Christmas."

"When are you going to leave?"

"I think I will head out in a couple of days."

"I know Wil will miss you, but I will miss you more. Life has been good for us since you came to town. I don't want to be without you."

Colin leaned over and kissed Mary. "I am falling in love with you, I am not going to let you go."

Mary stood up, "Let's go get something to eat."

Chapter 12

Colin woke up to a beam of morning light hitting his face through his bedroom window. A smile wrinkled his face as he sat up in his bed. He wanted to talk to Jake about an idea he had. He wanted to do it before he left town. He took a shower, dawned his clothes then walked to the back door of the restaurant. This will be the last time I will be doing this, he thought. He walked into the restaurant and sat at his usual spot in the back room. Dan placed a plate of his best breakfast goodies in front of him.

"I assume you will be leaving us today?" Dan asked.

"I will be," Colin replied.

Dan had a sad look in his eyes, "I have a feeling we won't see you again."

Colin smiled, "You can't get rid of me that easy."

Dan smiled, "Okay just as long as you promise you will be back."

"I promise!"

Colin finished his breakfast and cleaned his dishes, then walked out the front door, waiving at the girls in front. He walked across the street to Jed's General Store. He walked in the front door and was greeted by Jed, "Hey Colin, good to see you!"

Colin walked over to the tall lanky man and shook his hand. "I need to talk to you about something."

"Okay, let's go back to my office."

The two men walked back to Jed's office an sat down.

"What can I help you with Colin?" Jed asked.

"I have a proposition for you," Colin replied.

Jed looked at Colin with a quizzical face. "Okay"

"You know that Mayor Taylor has an investor for the ski resort. It looks like it's going to happen."

"Okay, what does that have to do with me?"

"Jed, you have the opportunity to get in on the ground floor of the new resort." Colin responded.

"What do you mean?" Jed asked.

"You are a businessman; you will have an opportunity to expand your business."

"You mean open another general store?"

"No, how about a ski shop. In the summer you could rent bicycles and such."

Jed looked at Colin for a moment then smiled, "okay and where am I supposed to get the money to do all of this. I like the idea, but everything I own is tied up in this business."

"Jed, I have a friend who invests in just this kind of thing."

Jed smiled, "You are a dishwasher who wanders. No offense, but who would you know that would invest that kind of money?"

Colin laughed, "I worked for a man who told me that if I saw a good investment while I was wandering, I should let him know."

Jed looked around his store, "I don't know anything about skiing or renting things. I am just a general store owner."

"I know you could do it. You hire people who know the business and I know you can do it. You could make a pot of money. Maybe enough to retire down the road."

"I think we are getting a little ahead of ourselves. I don't have the money yet. Let's see if your friend is willing to take a risk on an inexperienced storekeeper."

"So, you want me to get in touch with him?"

"I guess so. I have always wanted to expand, maybe this is the right ticket."

Colin shook Jed's hand, "Okay I will let him know. He will call you soon, I am sure."

Jed watched Colin as he went to the door, "I understand you are leaving us."

"I must go home for family business. I will be coming back."

Colin walked out the door and waived to Jed, "See you soon, Merry Christmas."

Colin walked quickly across the street to the Emporium. He wanted to say goodbye to the mayor. He entered the store, "Hi mayor!"

"Hi Colin, how are you?"

"I'm just fine, I wanted to wish you a Merry Christmas."

"Are you going somewhere?"

"I need to check in with my family, Christmas and all you know."

Mayor Taylor smiled, "I guess I thought you were alone, being a drifter. I thought you would be spending the holidays with us."

"I plan on coming back after Christmas. I love this community."

"What about Mary and Wil?"

"I plan on being with them."

Colin walked to the door, "Have a great Christmas. I will see you soon."

Colin walked down the street and took a deep breath. "I love it here." He pulled his phone out and dialed Williams.

"Mr. C, is everything all right?"

"Yes Williams, just fine. Can you send a car for me tonight? I will be waiting at the south end of town so no one will see me."

"Yes sir, I will be there personally. Should I bring anything?"

"No Williams, you will just be bringing me home."

"Oh, good sir, we have been worried about you. I should be there in an hour."

"Okay then I will see you soon." Colin hung up the phone and started walking to Mary's apartment. He knocked twice and Wil threw the door open and gave Colin a big hug.

"Hey, it's good to see you too." He patted Wil on the head. He walked to Mary and kissed her on the lips. "I missed you."

Mary hugged him and led him to the couch, "Are you leaving tonight?"

"Yes, I leave soon. I will see you for Christmas."

Wil stood in front of Colin, "You better be here. I am counting on you; you are going to bring Ben?"

"Yes, I will make sure Ben is with us. There is a surprise for you both tomorrow."

Wil perked up, "A surprise! What kind of surprise?"

"I can't tell you or it would not be a surprise." Colin and smiled.

Mary looked at Colin, "A surprise? Will you be bringing this surprise?"

"I can't tell you. Remember it's a surprise. Expect it around noon."

Colin stood up and moved to the door. Mary stood and walked with him. "Must you go?"

Colin hugged her and looked in her eyes, "I promise you will see me soon."

Mary smiled and kissed him, "I will expect to see you soon."

Colin opened the door and walked out to the porch, Mary was behind him and watched him walk down the steps and disappear in the dark. Once he was out of site Colin moved quickly to the south end of town. It was very dark as he walked down the street. Suddenly, lights flickered in the distance; It was Williams. Colin hurried to the car and got inside. He took a deep breath and exhaled.

"I am glad to see you, Williams."

"I am very glad to see you Mr. C."

Williams started the car and off they went.

Soon they were entering the gates of the house. The Christmas lights were all glowing.

"Williams you did a magnificent job on the lights."

"Thank you, sir, I wanted it to look as festive as possible. I know you wanted to give your new friends a wonderous Christmas."

"Williams, I am in love with this woman. Her son, Wil is a wonderful boy. I am planning on having them move in with us."

Williams looked back at Colin in the rearview mirror. "I am very happy for you sir. I have been hoping that you would find love again. What about the other little boy? I think you called him Ben."

"That is another story, Williams. This little boy lost his mother and father in a car accident. He is trying to adjust. He and I hit it off and I saw a spark in his eyes when we talked. He will be coming here for Christmas and if it all works out, I want to adopt him."

Williams stopped the car at the front door, jumped out and opened the door for Colin. Colin stepped inside and paused, taking in all the holiday decorations. The fire was crackling in the great room. Colin walked into the room and gazed at the twenty-foot Christmas tree. There were stockings hung off the mantle. Each one had a name written on it. Colin, Mary, Wil, and Ben. Colin smiled and walked to the kitchen. There was a wonderful smell floating from the oven in the corner. Chef John was working on some vegetables and stopped to greet Colin.

"It's good to have you back home, sir. I missed cooking for you."

"I missed your cooking, John. What are we having?"

John pointed to the oven, "for Christmas Eve dinner we are having English meat pies, vegetables, potatoes. Desert will be chocolate layer cake. For Christmas dinner we will have goose and all the fixings. Desert will be cherry pie and ice cream."

"Wow, that sounds great. I am looking forward to the feast." Colin left the kitchen and walked up the stairs to his room.

Chapter 13

Colin woke early, he was excited about the day to come. He hoped Mary would forgive him for not telling her who he was. He threw on his robe and walked downstairs. Williams was in the kitchen eating breakfast. "I need to talk to you about today."

"Yes sir, what can I do for you."

"I want you to have Mary, Wil and Ben picked up. I told Mary she would have a surprise at noon."

Williams looked at Colin, "A surprise sir?"

"Yes, they don't know who I am, I don't want them to know until they are here. So, when they are picked up, they are not to know where they are going. Tell them that Colin has a surprise for them, they need to go for a ride to see it. Make sure there are things to eat and drink for them."

Williams nodded his head, "Yes sir, I will have that taken care of right away."

Colin sat at the table with Williams, "I have an important mission for you. I have these envelopes to be dropped off to these people."

Williams looked at the names on the envelopes and looked at Colin, "I will deliver them myself. I will leave as soon as I get everything set up."

"What about presents for everyone tomorrow?"

"I have presents for both boys and the dress you wanted for Mary. Kathy picked up some other things she thought she might like."

"Thank you, Williams, I don't know how I would survive if you were not here to keep me on track."

Williams smiled, "I am happy to see you happy again sir."

Colin grabbed a cup of coffee and walked out into the great room. He thought about the days when he and his wife would sit in front of the fire and enjoy Christmas music.

Williams walked out to the garage and chose the Bentley to drive to Blue River. He wondered what the envelopes contained. After an hour he pulled up in front of the first address on an envelope. He looked up and the sign said, Blue River General Store. He walked into the store and up to the man at the counter. "I am looking for Jed Johnson."

"That's me. What can I do for you?"

"I have a special delivery for you."

Williams handed the envelope to the man and turned and walked out of the store. Jed was not sure about this mysterious man with an envelope. He opened the envelope and pulled a letter out.

The letter said:

Dear Jed,

I would be pleased to be your partner in a ski shop venture. I will front the money and you can run the shop. I will only ask for 10% of the net profit. I ask for no pay back.

Thank you for your friendship.

Merry Christmas,

Colin Wade

Jed put the letter on the counter and sat down. He could not believe his good fortune. He could not wait to tell his family. He closed up shop and hurried home.

Williams pulled up to the next address. It was the Emporium. There was a bustle of last-minute shoppers in and out of the store. Williams walked in the front door and looked around and walked up to an older woman at the counter.

"Can I help you," she asked.

Williams smiled, "Yes, I am looking for Millie Taylor."

"That is me. What is this about?"

"I have a delivery for you." Williams handed the envelope to her and turned, leaving the shop.

Millie watched as he left quickly. She opened the envelope and pulled the letter out. It said:

Dear Millie,

Merry Christmas! I look forward to working with you on the ski resort. I think it is a great idea and it will be a great benefit to the town and its people.

I ask one favor in return. I would like a five-acre lot near the resort where I can build my home. I will see you after the new year.

Your friend,

Colin Wade

Millie put the letter down and began to cry. I can't believe this is happening, this is the best Christmas present ever.

Williams pulled up to the next address. It was the orphanage. He walked up the long stone stairs, knocked on the door. A small child answered the door, "Is Susan here?"

The little girl looked at Williams and said, "Yes."

"Would you give this to her?"

The little girl took the envelope and closed the door. Williams laughed. Off to the next address. The little girl ran to Susan and handed the envelope to her. She looked at the little girl and asked, "Where did this come from?"

The little girl looked at her, "The man at the door gave it to me. He said give it to you."

Susan looked at the envelope and walked to her cramped office. She tore the envelope open. She read:

Dear Susan,

Thanks for your dedication to these children. Without you their lives would be empty. I want you to know that I will be funding the remodel of the house and addition of an office, as well as anything you might need to make life better for you and the children.

At 8PM tonight a truck will drive up in your driveway. The truck is full of gifts for you and the children. The men on the truck will help you unload the gifts and set them under the tree. Just make sure they are in bed, so they don't see Santa.

Your friend,

Colin Wade

Millie began to weep. One of the children heard her and asked her if she was all right. She smiled, "I think Santa has come to our home."

One last stop for Williams. It was the restaurant. Williams walked into the bustling establishment and asked for Dan. The girl at the counter called out for Dan. He walked out of the back room and up to Williams. "What can I do for you?"

"I have a delivery for you." He handed the envelope to Dan and quickly left the shop.

Dan looked at the envelope and with great curiosity opened the envelope. He pulled the letter out and several checks fell out. The letter said:

Dan,

Merry Christmas to you and the staff. I look forward to doing business with you in the future. Please see that all the girls and the guys in the kitchen get these checks.

Thank you, my friend,

Colin Wade

Dan looked at the checks. Each person was to receive one thousand dollars. Dan passed out the checks and everybody began to dance. Each one said Merry Christmas from Colin. Dan just had a glazed look. They all asked how this could happen. The Sheriff was sitting at the counter.

"Colin Wade is a billionaire. He didn't want anybody to know. He purchased all the new patrol cars for the department."

Dan just sat down, "I can't believe he kept it a secret."

They all quickly looked out the window, just in time to see the taillights of the Bentley.

Williams smiled as he drove back to the estate. He knew what was going on. Colin was completing the legacy of his wife.

Colin walked into his closet and scanned his clothes. I will wear something casual today he thought. I want my guests to feel comfortable here. The car to pick them up should almost be there.

A large limousine pulled up in front of the small apartment of Mary and Wil. A stately man exited the car and walked to the door. He knocked twice and the door opened. Mary stood there and looked at the man.

"I am Philip, I am here to pick you up. I have a letter here to explain."

Mary opened the letter:

Philip is here to take you to your surprise. Please pack an overnight bag and Philip will take care of the rest.

Love,

Colin

Mary smiled, "Will you come in?"

Philip tipped his hat, "I will wait at the car ma'am."

Mary closed the door and just then Wil came from his room. "Who was that? Was that Colin?"

"No, but it is the surprise Colin promised. Go pack your small suitcase for an overnight stay."

Wil was excited, "Maybe we are going to his house."

"I don't know but you better hurry because there is a man waiting outside for us."

Wil dashed to the window and looked out. "There is a big limousine out front. Is that for us?"

"Yes, it's for us, so hurry and get packed."

Mary and Wil climbed into the back seat of the limousine while Philip placed the luggage in the trunk. Wil was greeted by Ben. They were both excited when he saw the game controller and a small screen. They saw some soda and chips. They both thought they was in heaven. Mary saw a bottle of wine and some cheese and crackers. Philip got into the front seat and rolled the privacy screen down.

"I hope everything is to your liking. We have about an hour drive to our destination."

Mary was still confused, "I guess I don't understand where we are going?"

"I was told that I was to drive you to your surprise."

Wil piped up, "Remember Colin told us that he had a surprise for us."

Mary smiled at Wil, "I guess you are right. We should enjoy the surprise."

The time passed quickly. The two boys played video games. Soon the car turned off the main road and onto a small country road. It was beautiful here Mary thought as they drove on. The trees were thick, the snow covered everything. Soon the car slowed and turned onto what looked like a long driveway. After five minutes Mary could see a house on a hill in the distance. It was beautiful she thought. Maybe it is an Inn, we will be staying there. Mary could not believe that Colin could afford this, but maybe it is just a stop on the way to the surprise.

Soon they were at a large iron gate with the letter "W" on it. The gate slowly opened; the limo drove through. Wil and Ben looked out the window and could see that everything was decorated for Christmas. It was still too light out to see the lights, but it looked beautiful. The limo came to a stop in front of the large castle like building. It was composed of stone and brick. Two large wood doors with the letter "W" on them opened slowly. A man dressed like a butler stepped out and opened the limo door, Wil and Mary stepped out.

"Hello, I am Williams. Please follow me and I will show you to your rooms."

Mary, Wil, and Ben followed Williams into the estate. It was beautiful inside. Everything was decorated for Christmas. It looked like something out of a movie Mary thought. Up a set of stair and then to the first door. Williams stopped.

"This your room ma'am."

Williams opened the door. The room was as big as their apartment. A huge bed at the center of the room. The bathroom was covered in marble, with a large soaking tub near the window.

Mary was stunned, "This is mine?"

"Yes ma'am. Is everything alright?"

"Are you sure this is mine?

"Williams smiled, "Yes, mam. Mr. Wil's and Ben's room is right next door."

Wil and Ben ran to the next door and opened it. The room was huge. It was decorated with all kinds of hockey memorabilia. Wil just stood there and staired. "Wow!" Ben ran to a small Christmas tree near the window.

"Look, we have our own tree!"

Another man dressed like a butler brought their luggage to their rooms and made sure they were settled.

Williams stepped out of Mary's room, "If you would like to take a moment to freshen up then come downstairs to the great room, there will be a surprise for you."

Colin was nervous. I hope they will forgive me for not telling them the truth, he thought. Williams came downstairs and saw Colin sitting in his chair.

"Are you alright sir?"

"I don't know Williams. Do you think they will forgive me for not be honest?"

Williams laughed, "I don't think you have anything to worry about sir."

Soon Colin could hear footsteps on the stairs. It was Ben and Wil. They both ran immediately to Colin, Jumping into his lap.

"Wow, this is great they both yelled!"

Colin could hear Mary coming down the stairs and stood up. The boys ran to the Christmas tree. Mary walked into the room and saw Colin standing there. Colin moved quickly to Mary and embraced her.

"I am so glad you re here."

Mary kissed him and stepped back, "How can you afford to put us up in the beautiful Inn?"

Colin smiled, "Why don't you all take a seat. I have a confession to make."

They all sat on the large leather couch looking at Colin with a blank face.

"I haven't been honest with all of you. I am not a dishwasher. This is my house."

Mary shook her head. "I don't understand."

"Ok, after my wife died, I lost the drive to live. I went into a shell and didn't come out. One day I decided to get out and see life again. My wife was very giving, I thought that I could find my way back if I looked for a reason to go on. I found it in Blue River. I didn't want people to know who I was, so I pretended to be a drifter. That is where it all began."

Mary stood up, "Who are you?"

"I am Colin Wade. You saw the "W" on the gate and doors. This is my house. I am a retired businessman. I own property all over the country. I still have a staff to help me run my day-to-day life. I am very wealthy."

Ben stood up, "Are you a millionaire?"

Colin laughed, "I have a little more than a million. Just put a "B" at the beginning of that word."

Ben scratched his head, "'B'?"

Wil pipped up, "He is a billionaire!"

Mary sat back down on the couch. Her face was flush. "I can't believe this."

Colin walked over to Mary, "Will you forgive me for not telling the truth? This was the surprise"

Wil jumped up, "I forgive you!"

Ben, "Me too!"

Mary was still in shock and sat there for a moment. "Why did you think you couldn't tell me?"

"I didn't want to burden you with that secret."

Mary looked up at Colin. "Were you the person who paid the hospital bills?"

"Yes."

"What about the new car?"

"Yes."

"Why did you do all of this?"

Colin sat next to Mary. "I started my wandering with the intent to make others lives better. When I saw what you were going through, I knew you needed help. I tried to help several people in town. I didn't expect to fall in love with you."

Wil looked at Mary, "Mom, I think he loves you; I think you love him."

Colin put his arm around Mary and kissed her cheek. Mary turned and kissed Colin on the lips.

Colin stood up, "Okay, there is food in the dining room, so let's go eat."

The boys jumped up and ran into the dining room and sat at the table. Colin and Mary walked in behind them.

"How about after we eat, we go outside and look at the lights? We can even sing some Christmas carols."

The boys both responded, "Yeah!"

The lights came on and they all sat and enjoyed the evening. Soon, it was time to go to bed.

"Ok, let's hit the hay boys. Santa won't stop here until you are asleep."

You didn't need to tell them twice. They yelled good night as they ran up the stairs. Mary kisses Colin passionately before she walked up to her room. Colin smiled and sat back down on the couch. Williams came into the room. "Sir, should I place the presents under the tree now?"

"Yes, I can help if you would like?"

"I will take of it sir. Besides, the staff looks forward to doing this."

Colin patted Williams on the shoulder to say thank you.

Everyone fell asleep quickly. Morning came early with the voices of excited boys filled the house. Soon a knock came on Colins door.

"Colin get up, Santa came, we are all waiting downstairs!"

Colin got up and threw his robe on and walked down the stairs to the great room. Everyone was standing looking at the tree and the piles of presents under the tree. The boys immediately grabbed the bicycles and jumped on them. Mary turned to look at Colin. She was wearing the red silk robe Colin left in her room.

"Thank you for the beautiful robe."

"You are welcome. Go and open the other gifts. Boys check out your stockings by the fire. Bring your mothers over to her."

Ben handed Mary a small Christmas stocking and she pulled out a small box with a bow on it. She opened the box. It was the neckless that he purchased at the Emporium. The note inside said, 'I love you.'

Mary walked to Colin and threw her arms around his neck, "I love you very much."

The boys were thrashing the presents and squealing with excitement. Mary opened her gifts and kissed Colin after each one.

"I have a gift for you," Mary stated.

Colin had a quizzical look on his face. Mary handed him a small box and a card. The card was made by Wil. Colin read the card and thanked Wil. He opened the gift. It was his name tag from the restaurant. Colin began to laugh, "I will cherish this forever. Thank you."

Williams was standing by the dining room door. Colin motioned to him. "I have something for you and the staff."

Colin handed several envelopes to Williams. "Thank You sir," Williams responded. "I will make sure everyone gets their envelope."

Colin motioned again to Williams, "You are a part of the family Williams, come and join us while we open our gifts. You can open yours too."

Williams was humbled. He took a seat near the fireplace and opened his envelope. His eyes began to tear up as he read the note. Then he saw the check in the envelope. "Sir, I cannot take this. It is too much."

"Nonsense Williams, you deserve every penny."

Mary leaned over to Colin and whispered, "What did you give him?"

Colin whispered back, "Twenty thousand."

Mary just smiled. The boys were playing with their toys and were deep in pleasure. Colin stood up.

"Can I have all of your attention!"

Everybody stopped what they were doing and looked at Colin.

"I have an announcement. I have never been happier than right now. I would like this to keep going. I would ask you if you would like to come and live with me here?

Ben stood up, "What about me?"

Colin walked over to Ben, "I don't know. Do you all think Ben should live here?"

Wil immediately stated, "I want him to stay here!"

Colin laughed, "Well, if it's okay with you Ben, I have already started adoption proceedings. I would love for you to be a part of this family."

Ben turned and wrapped his arms around Colin's waist.

Wil yelled yeah and Mary smiled. Colin walked to the couch and sat next to Mary. Colin whispered in Mary's ear. "I want you and Wil to be part of this family too." Colin pulled a small box from his robe. "Will you marry me?"

Mary looked at Colin, "I would love to be your wife."

Colin immediately stood up, "Hey gang, Mary just agreed to marry me!"

Everyone met in the middle of the room with a group hug. Colin had realized that his life was going to keep moving forward. He would be happy again. The Christmas Angel visited him too.

THE END

Merry Christmas